CHOSEN

teddekker.com

DEKKER FANTASY

BOOKS OF HISTORY CHRONICLES

THE LOST BOOKS (YOUNG ADULT)
Chosen
Infidel
Renegade
Chaos
Lunatic (WITH KACI HILL)
Elyon (WITH KACI HILL)

THE CIRCLE SERIES
Green
Black
Red
White

THE PARADISE BOOKS
Showdown
Saint
Sinner

Skin
House (WITH FRANK PERETTI)

DEKKER MYSTERY

Immanuel's Veins (COMING SEPTEMBER 2010)
Blink of an Eye
Kiss (WITH ERIN HEALY)
Burn (WITH ERIN HEALY)

MARTYR'S SONG SERIES
Heaven's Wager
When Heaven Weeps
Thunder of Heaven
The Martyr's Song

THE CALEB BOOKS
Blessed Child
A Man Called Blessed

DEKKER THRILLER

THR3E
Obsessed
Adam

CHOSEN

LOST BOOK 1

TED DEKKER

THOMAS NELSON
Since 1798

NASHVILLE   DALLAS   MEXICO CITY   RIO DE JANEIRO

Published in Nashville, Tennessee, by Thomas Nelson. Thomas Nelson is a registered trademark of Thomas Nelson, Inc.

Thomas Nelson, Inc. books may be purchased in bulk for educational, business, fund-raising, or sales promotional use. For information, please e-mail SpecialMarkets@ThomasNelson.com.

Publisher's Note: This novel is a work of fiction. Names, characters, places, and incidents are either products of the author's imagination or used fictitiously. All characters are fictional, and any similarity to people living or dead is purely coincidental.

Cover Design by The DesignWorks Group, Inc.
Page Design by Casey Hooper
Map Design by Chris Ward

ISBN 978-1-59554-859-7 (TP)

Library of Congress Cataloging-in-Publication Data

Dekker, Ted, 1962-
  Chosen / Ted Dekker.
     p. cm. — (The circle series ; bk. 1)
  ISBN: 978-1-59554-359-2
  I. Title.
PS3554.E43C47 2007
813'.54--dc22

                                                                    2007032976

Printed in the United States of America
10 11 12 13 14 RRD 5 4 3 2 1

BEGINNINGS

Our story begins in a world totally like our own, yet completely different. What once happened here in our own history seems to be repeating itself thousands of years from now, some time beyond the year 4000 AD.

But this time the future belongs to those who see opportunity before it becomes obvious. To the young, to the warriors, to the lovers. To those who can follow hidden clues and find a great treasure that will unlock the mysteries of life and wealth.

Thirteen years have passed since the lush, colored forests were turned to desert by Teeleh, the enemy of Elyon and the vilest of all creatures. Evil now rules the land and shows itself as a painful, scaly disease that covers the flesh of the Horde, a people who live in the desert.

The powerful green waters, once precious to Elyon, have vanished from the earth except in seven small forests surrounding seven small lakes. Those few who have chosen to follow the ways of Elyon now live in these forests, bathing once daily in the powerful waters to cleanse their skin of the disease.

The number of their sworn enemy, the Horde, has grown in thirteen years and, fearing the green waters above all else, these desert dwellers have sworn to wipe all traces of the forests from the earth.

Only the Forest Guard stands in their way. Ten thousand elite fighters against an army of nearly four hundred thousand Horde.

But the Forest Guard is starting to crumble.

ONE

DAY ONE

Qurong, general of the Horde, stood on the tall dune five miles west of the green forest, ignoring the fly that buzzed around his left eye.

His flesh was nearly white, covered with a paste that kept his skin from itching too badly. His long hair was pulled back and woven into dreadlocks, then tucked beneath the leather body armor cinched tightly around his massive chest.

"Do you think they know?" the young major beside him asked.

Qurong's milky white horse, chosen for its ability to blend with the desert, stamped and snorted.

The general spit to one side. "They know what we want them

3

to know," he said. "That we are gathering for war. And that we will march from the east in four days."

"It seems risky," the major said. His right cheek twitched, sending three flies to flight.

"Their forces are half what they once were. As long as they think we are coming from the east, we will smother them from the west."

"The traitor insists that they are building their forces," the major said.

"With young pups!" Qurong scoffed.

"The young can be crafty."

"And I'm not? They know nothing about the traitor. This time we will kill them all."

Qurong turned back to the valley behind him. The tents of his third division, the largest of all Horde armies, which numbered well over three hundred thousand of the most experienced warriors, stretched out nearly as far as he could see.

"We march in four days," Qurong said. "We will slaughter them from the west."

TWO

Twelve of the forest's strongest and bravest young fighters crouched in their brown battle leathers at each end of the grassy stadium field, waiting for the command to stand and fight for the hairy ball sitting at center field. Five thousand spectators stood in the stands carved from the earth, holding their collective breath. Four squad leaders were to be chosen today, and each one given a house to own, the choice of any horse, and an emerald-handled sword—making them the envy of every man, woman, and child in the village.

All of this would be decided by one man: Thomas Hunter, supreme commander of the Forest Guard.

Johnis stood next to his father, Ramos, shivering a little. It wasn't cold, but the breeze dried the sweat on his neck and made him cool. So he told himself, anyway.

He had dark hair to his shoulders and, according to his father, a strong jaw that was sometimes best kept closed. His nose was sharp and his lips full, giving him the appearance that he was fourteen, not sixteen.

He stared at the hairy Horde ball at center field. His mother, Rosa, had been responsible for that lump of Scab hair. Three months had passed since she'd been killed by the Horde at the forest's edge while searching for a special plant, the catalina cactus, whose herbal power might've healed a fever that had come over Johnis. The Forest Guard had been to the north in battle, but she'd refused to wait for an escort while her boy suffered.

His mother had always been like that, dropping everything on his account. Sweet Mother, with her long, dark hair and ruby lips.

Mother, why did you go? Please forgive me, dear Mother.

Johnis had thrown himself on the ground and wailed for the whole village to hear. His father had left the forest in a rage and returned with the long, tangled hair from ten Horde he'd killed that very afternoon—the makings of that hairy Horde ball on the field now.

But nothing eased the pain in Johnis's chest.

Two weeks ago Thomas Hunter had announced the decision to lower the Forest Guard's recruitment age from eighteen to sixteen. He was looking to boost the fighting force by one thousand. The forests had erupted in debate.

Those who had protested had cried in fear at the thought of their sons and daughters entering battle against the Horde. They all knew that the Forest Guard was outnumbered ten to one. They knew that every time the Guard went to battle, many died. They knew that the weakest, their sons and daughters, would die first.

But the people of the forest also knew that the Horde had sworn to kill them all. All living followers of Elyon knew, whether or not they admitted it publicly, that the fate of the Forest Dwellers rested squarely on the shoulders of the youngest fighters now joining the Forest Guard.

All sixteen- and seventeen-year-olds worth their salt had then signed up to be considered. With his mother's death fresh in his mind, Johnis had been one of the first in line. The Guard had dismissed all but two thousand, from which they would select the final thousand fighters.

Johnis was one of those who'd been dismissed. Too small, they said. He was just barely sixteen and still too wounded from his mother's death. Maybe next time, if there was a next time.

"What do you say, Johnis?" his father whispered. "Who is the strongest?"

Johnis scanned the players in this game Thomas Hunter called *football*—a name that supposedly came from his dreams of another land. All twenty-four were already mighty fighters, even though none was older than seventeen. Roughly half were women, and of those Johnis thought maybe Darsal was the strongest. Not the largest, but the strongest. And very quick.

She crouched fewer than fifty feet from where Johnis stood on the sidelines. Her fingers were wrapped tightly around the same three-foot fighting stick they had all been given. Muscles rippled up her arm, glistening with sweat. The side of her sleeveless tunic was stained with a little blood—it was, after all, a full-contact sport. Within thirty days the recruits would be swinging razor-sharp swords in full battle against the Horde. No one dared enter the Forest Guard fearful of a little blood when so much more was at stake.

Her long, brown hair was tucked under a leather helmet and had been pulled back into a ponytail, showing a strong, smooth jawline to her ear on the right side of her face. A terrible scar marked her left—a burn that forced Johnis to stare and wonder what had put it there. It made her more fearsome than ugly. Whatever had caused the wound had also gotten her left shoulder, although her leather armor covered most of the scar there.

The Horde had killed her father. Johnis could practically see the thirst for revenge in her squinting eyes. But something else had happened to make her stick close to Billos, another fighter in contention for the top spot today. They were from the same forest and were clearly very close. At first Johnis had assumed they were brother and sister, but no.

"What do you say, lad?" his father asked again.

"Darsal," he said, in a whisper that sounded hoarse.

His father grunted. "Now *there's* a choice. She'd make any man a fine wife." He glanced down at Johnis. "A little more muscle on those bones and you could make a play for her yet, boy. Though she seems a bit stuck on the other youngster."

His father nudged him, and Johnis gave him a weak smile.

Father could not know that his frequent comparisons with those who'd been selected to try out for the Forest Guard bothered him. The honor of wearing the hardened leather breastplates, wielding the Guard swords and whips, riding the best horses, being watched by everyone else as you walked down the path on your way to battle—who wouldn't trade his life for a chance to be called one of the Forest Guard?

Who, besides Johnis? Truly, he wasn't sure he would make a good fighter in bloody battle. In fact, he was quite sure he wouldn't.

Still, Father's small comments made Johnis feel weak, reminding him that he stood on the sidelines because he wasn't worthy. He shifted on his feet and crossed his arms over his chest, hugging himself.

Thomas Hunter paced across the field. There wasn't a man or woman among them who wouldn't be honored to kiss the commander's hand. The Forest Guard had saved the forests many times, and Thomas Hunter was the reason for it all.

He slid his emerald-handled sword from its metal sheath, filling the stadium with the sound of steel scraping steel. Perfect silence settled on the crowd.

Thomas swung the sword absently, neatly cutting the grass at his feet in an arc.

"Is this all I can expect from you?" his voice rang out. He jabbed the air with his sword. "I'm looking for four leaders to step forward and show they are worthy to stand by my side."

No one responded. What Thomas could be looking for that he hadn't already seen was beyond Johnis.

"Take a look around," Thomas shouted. He slowly swung his sword across the stadium. "The fate of every man, woman, and child in this arena will be in the hands of the Forest Guard. And you say you want to *lead* that Guard? You are all either mad or complete fools, because I don't see a leader in the lot."

He paced back to the sideline, studying the line of twelve on his right, then the line on his left. Behind him the ball of hair lay undisturbed.

To win, one team had to run to the middle, pick up the ball, and cross the other team's goal line. What seemed simple enough was made very difficult by the fact that the other team was armed with fighting sticks.

The day had started with a hundred of the most promising recruits. Seventy-six had been dismissed, seventeen of them on stretchers.

It was down to these two teams of twelve each.

Thomas raised his sword high, then swung it down hard. "Go!"

The two lines of recruits silently bolted from where they crouched and raced toward the ball on a collision course.

THREE

For a count of five, the only sound Johnis could hear was the thudding of feet as the two lines sprinted for each other. Silvie, the wiry fireball with short blond hair, was the first to reach the ball.

She'd just scooped it up when the lines collided with a tremendous thud. Then the sound of sticks smashing filled the stadium with bone-jarring cracks.

The crowd erupted in a roar of support that smothered the grunts of the contestants. The leafy trees surrounding the oval amphitheater seemed to shake on all sides, sending birds scattering for cover. Possums, lizards, rodents, and smaller animals of all shapes and sizes ran into their holes as if they knew that their future, too, was at stake in this game.

Silvie ducked under a vicious swing from a fighter named Jackov, the largest and clearly the strongest one on the field. She came up under his extended arm with her own stick, but Jackov was too skilled to be fooled so easily. He deflected her weapon with the shield on his left arm and knocked the ball loose with his knee. The football flew high, then landed in the tangle of bodies, lost from sight.

"Think!" Thomas screamed. "Use your heads! For the sake of Elyon, use your heads!"

If the players on the field were not all highly skilled at deflecting blows with their leather-wrapped forearms, they would undoubtedly all be dead, Johnis thought. *They would at least be a pile of broken bones.*

"Better to break an arm here among friends than have your head cut off in the desert," Thomas cried to all who protested the brutal fighting. These were desperate times, and they called for desperate measures.

Billos, the seventeen-year-old snake-quick fighter who was known as "the bulldog," slid out of the mess and ran around the sparring teams, searching for the ball.

He darted in, snatched something near Darsal's feet, took two steps toward the opposite goal, and came face-to-face with Jackov. The big boy swung his stick at Billos's chest. The wood landed with a blow that rose over the crowd noise.

Thud!

Johnis winced. The stadium fell silent except for a few clacking sticks.

Billos stood his ground, stunned, ball gripped in his left fist.

Seeing Billos hurt, Jackov dove in for the kill.

"Head butt!" Darsal screamed.

Instead of dodging, as Johnis expected him to, Billos tossed the football in Darsal's direction, lowered his head, and stepped into the onrushing opponent.

But Jackov sidestepped Billos's helmeted head and snatched the flying ball from the air before it reached Darsal.

Billos flew past him, hit the ground, and rolled to his feet.

Before Jackov could head for the goal line, Silvie grabbed his right ear from behind. She yanked back, slamming the boy on his back.

Then twenty-four bodies dove at the loose ball. They were all so bunched up, so tangled and intertwined, that no one had room to swing, much less take the time required to think through any strategy.

And the ball was lost in that pile.

Thomas paced like a lion and let them fight, but he wasn't happy. And no wonder: a fight like this with the Horde would get them all killed.

Some said the only way the Forest Dwellers could survive would be to make peace with the Horde, but they said it in a whisper because such cowardly talk could get a person killed. Only traitors would dare say it publicly.

But watching the mess on the field, Johnis wasn't sure a battle led by any of these sixteen- or seventeen-year-old fawns would be better than surrender. They looked like one huge ball of hair themselves.

Something shot out from the pile and bounced across the grass toward the sideline. It was the ball of Horde hair, the football.

All would have been fine if the ball had stopped on the field. But it didn't. It kept rolling. Toward Johnis.

He was sure it would stop as it passed Thomas, but it kept rolling.

Still toward Johnis.

Every eye in the stadium followed the lumpy brown sphere. Johnis glanced up at Thomas and saw that his eyes, too, were on the ball. When he looked back down, the football had stopped. At his feet.

One look at the field and Johnis saw that the fighting had only intensified.

"Fools will get us all killed," his father said, bending to pick up the ball. He grabbed it with a thick, cracked fist, lifted it, then stopped.

"Throw it out," Johnis said. "Hurry!"

Instead, his father dropped the ball. It bounced once and landed on Johnis's left foot, where it rested.

"What are you doing?" Johnis asked, glancing up at his father. But Ramos's eyes were on Thomas.

Johnis looked down at the ball. A picture that had haunted his dreams flashed through his mind: an image of ten huge Horde warriors—"Scabs," as the Forest Guard called them— killing his mother. This was their hair! It made him suddenly sick. He froze.

"Stop!" Thomas Hunter's voice roared above the sounds of fighting. "On your feet!"

Jackov was already standing, storming toward the crowd at Johnis's right. He was hunting for the ball, Johnis realized. The boy's face was red from fighting, and his eyes glared with anger.

"Give it up," Jackov growled, eyes scanning the crowd.

Whether it was the image of his mother or the sight of the furious Jackov, Johnis didn't know, but he moved without thinking. He slipped his foot around the ball and eased it behind his heels so that it was hidden from view.

"Give it up!" Jackov thundered, pacing along the sideline closer to Johnis. The other fighters had stood and were watching.

"You've lost the ball and you think a few words will bring it back?" Thomas called.

Johnis's heart thumped. He almost kicked it out then. But he didn't.

"Use your head!" Thomas said, facing the others. "All of you, listen to me. How many times have I told you that you must defeat the Horde with what's in your head and your heart before you defeat them with your muscle? They outnumber us! They outmuscle us! They are stronger, but we have more heart. So think with your heart!"

His voice rang out with enough force to bring a tremble to Johnis's legs.

"Let them see the confidence in your eyes. Let them know that your heart cannot be stopped! I need leaders who will stand in the face of terror and laugh. I need a few who will throw their heads back and roar at the sun because they know that Elyon is on their side, and no one, not even the smelly Horde, can defeat the followers of Elyon!"

Encouraged by Thomas's speech, Jackov screamed at the crowd. "Give up the Horde hair or I swear I will slit your throat where you stand!"

Is this what Thomas meant? Johnis wondered.

"Use your head, Jackov!" Thomas shouted, egging the fighter on. "Find me my football!"

Jackov began to run along the sideline, joined now by three others from his team.

"An extra horse to the one who finds my ball!" Thomas challenged.

Now ten of the twenty-four ran to the sidelines, slapping their palms with sticks.

Johnis felt sweat running down his neck. Why was the crowd so silent? He'd done a foolish thing, hiding the ball. Why wasn't his father scooping the ball up and throwing it out before any of the fighters discovered that it had been him, Johnis, who'd hidden it from them?

Then Thomas winked at him, and he knew what was happening. The commander was using him to make a point. *Even a weak boy, rejected from consideration to join the Guard, can hide a ball from you.*

"Stop!"

They stopped. All but Jackov, who required more urging.

"Stop or take the back of my hand, boy."

Now Jackov stopped.

"Use your heads," Thomas said, pacing again. "I said I want you to find my Horde football. It was a special gift, and I have no intention of losing it."

He faced Darsal. "Darsal, do you think the football has vanished? Plucked from us by a beast in the sky?"

"No, sir. It's being hidden by someone along the side."

"Then why are you standing in the middle of the field?" Thomas asked.

"Because as soon as your football is found, there will be another fight," she said. "I'm resting."

Thomas hesitated, then nodded. He looked at Billos. "And you?"

"I plan to retrieve the football for you, sir," Billos replied.

"Is that so? By standing there in the middle with Darsal, resting?"

Billos glanced at Darsal but said nothing.

Thomas shifted his attention to Silvie, the short blond who'd reached the ball first. They said she was an intelligent one, given to schooling before she lost her mother and took up fighting. All Johnis could see was speed and power and a firm jaw. She was a quiet girl.

"And you, Silvie?" Thomas asked.

"If I thought stomping around the field like a spoiled child would get me the ball, I still wouldn't bother," she said.

"Then you don't care about my football? I, your supreme leader, have offered you an extra horse if you can find it, and you stand as if you don't care?"

"Begging your pardon, sir," Silvie said, dipping her head. "But you're right, I *don't* care about your Horde football. In fact, I find it a bit disgusting. And I think there are a thousand boys who will offer me their horses after today."

This was the most Johnis had heard her say in all the days he'd watched them spar. She was the loner on the field, like him in some ways.

"You're not married yet?" Thomas asked.

"No." Even though sixteen was an acceptable marrying age, marriage was discouraged among new recruits.

"Sixteen or seventeen?"

"Sixteen, sir," Silvie said.

They all knew Thomas would make his selection as much on how they answered his questions as on how well they fought. He was obsessed with this thinking stuff. Head and heart, head and heart, head and heart, it was more head and heart than strength, he often said.

Thomas turned to Jackov, who was still scanning the sidelines and hunting for the ball. The only reason he hadn't spotted the sphere of hair behind Johnis was because of Ramos's larger boot blocking part of the view.

"Jackov?" Thomas demanded.

It has come down to these four, Johnis thought. Thomas had chosen two men and two women.

"I would have found your football, sir, but you stopped me," Jackov said.

"I don't remember stopping you," Thomas said.

"You ordered me to stop," Jackov protested.

"I also ordered you to find my football, which you failed to do in a timely manner," Thomas said. "Then I suggested you come to your senses or take the back of my hand. But you know the rules: there *are* no rules in matters of wit and mind. Yet you blame me for your not having the ball in your hands at this very moment?"

"Then let me resume my search," Jackov said as he bowed.

"I intend to. As soon as I give Billos a chance."

Thomas turned in a slow circle and spoke loudly so that the thousands gathered heard every word. "And when you do find my Horde football, Jackov or Billos or whoever manages the task by might or mind, I want you to beat that single soul who has hidden my Horde football to a pulp."

Silence echoed.

"Do you hear me?"

"Yes, sir," Jackov said.

"Just enough to teach them a lesson," Thomas said. "Enough to break a bone or two."

"Yes, sir."

"And if they try to squirm out of it now, I will personally break a bone or two," Thomas said.

Johnis's heart pounded with panic.

FOUR

The day had taken a terrible turn for the worse, and Johnis was out of options. He had always been known for two things: his love of words and his impulsiveness. What so many thought of as an odd combination seemed perfectly natural to Johnis. But at the moment, he doubted running impulsively from the stadium in blind panic would make his day any better.

That left words, and the only words Johnis could think of at the moment were, *The Horde ball is a trick.*

Johnis didn't have time to think through the reason or likelihood these words might help him out; he just spoke them on instinct, knowing that something in his head thought it was a good idea, if a bit juvenile.

So he pulled his father down by his sleeve and whispered into his ear, "The Horde ball is a trick. Pass it on to save my life."

"What?"

"Pass it on to save my life—the Horde ball is a trick."

His father gave him a short, strange look, then leaned to his neighbor, Thelma, a seamstress who made leather goods for the Guard, and whispered into her ear. She in turn whispered into her neighbor's ear. And around it went.

"So, Billos," Thomas was saying, "will you agree to beat the one who's hiding the Horde ball to a pulp if you uncover him?"

"Consider it done," Billos said.

"Then have at it."

By now the whispering had gone a quarter of the way around the stadium and had gathered some attention. Five or six people sharing a secret was easy to hide, but this secret was passed on and on, gathering more and more looks from those around. Even some of the fighters had noticed.

Billos scanned the crowd and called out for all to hear. "My friends, as you can see here, I will soon be serving in the Guard, which means I will be offering my life to protect yours."

Johnis guessed that Billos meant to ask the crowd to turn him in.

Billos noticed the whispering and glanced to his right, by the far goal, where a man was bending to a shorter woman, passing on the secret. Most of the fighters had followed Billos's eyes and were watching with some curiosity.

"In exchange for my life, I would like to ask one thing only," Billos continued.

Johnis moved quickly, while their attention was diverted. He slipped the knife from his father's belt, squatted down over the ball, and quickly sawed at the main cord that held the long strands of hair tight. Sweat streamed down his cheeks.

The cord around the ball snapped easily, thank Elyon.

Johnis dropped the knife, turned so that his back was toward the field, and stood, holding the Horde ball in his hands.

Horde warriors never cut their hair, preferring instead to weave it into long, nasty dreadlocks. The hair was greasy in his hands as he fumbled with one of the knots. It smelled like sulfur.

Still, considering the predicament he was in, he might have swallowed the whole ball of hair if it would save him from a beating.

Then again, who was to say that Billos could really beat him in a fight? Johnis was no stranger to swinging a sword.

Then yet again, Billos was stronger.

The knot loosed, and the hair unraveled. Johnis wrapped it around his hips, slid it up to his waist, tucked each end under his belt, and pulled his shirt over it. He slowly turned around.

"I pledge my life," Billos was saying. "Offer me the ball, my friend, and I'll go easy on the beating I've been ordered to give you. It's the least you can do."

No one on the field appeared to have noticed Johnis. Who could resist a whispered secret? No one. A mild but effective distraction. Now he had the Horde hair hidden around his belly.

The murmurs and chuckling of those around him might give him away. His father had already thought of that. "Shut up!" he snapped at those behind.

They quieted.

Billos called to an old man who'd just been whispered to by a girl. "You there, old man. Step out."

He did.

"What did she tell you?" Billos asked.

"She told me, 'I'm bored and sick.'"

"Bored and sick?" Billos repeated.

"This talk is making us all bored and sick," the old man said. "Get on with the fight, boy!"

"The Horde ball is a trick" had become "I'm bored and sick," Johnis realized. Laughter rippled softly through the crowd, and his tension eased a little. Maybe this would all work out.

Then again, there was that "beat him to a pulp" thing.

Elyon, by the mercy of the Roush, save me, he pleaded, referring to the stories of the white bats that had once protected them from Teeleh and the evil Shataiki bats. None had been seen in thirteen years, but some said the shrieks of the black bats could be heard in the desert night.

The legends didn't matter at the moment, but Johnis could use a miracle. Some of the power of old.

A little magic, maybe.

But there was no magic. Not here, not now. There was just him with smelly Horde hair wrapped around his bare, sweating belly.

How had he managed to get into such an absurd situation? Quick thinking could save your life or end it, Thomas was known to say.

Johnis was the king of quick thinkers.

Billos swung around, gazing at the crowd and wearing a grin. "I must say, I have to agree. It's all become a bit boring and sick to me as well. Some fool has gone off and hidden the ball and won't give it back. Fine, let's try something else. All those who think that the fool who is hiding Thomas's Horde hair ball should give himself up, step forward and be counted."

Without pausing to consider precisely why it made perfect sense, Johnis stepped out. It did make sense, of course. Perfect sense. The best defense was always an aggressive offense. So said Thomas Hunter.

Billos faced him. "Good, one boy who knows the meaning of honor. A small boy without much meat on his bones, but more courage than the rest. Is he the only one?"

Almost as one the entire first row of onlookers stepped out to form a ring around the stadium.

Billos glanced at Darsal. "Check behind them."

Darsal took off in a jog, running behind the row that had stepped out, scanning the ground and bleachers for the ball.

"This is absurd!" Jackov cried out. "Give me my way and I'll find you your Horde football, sir."

Darsal finished her loop and rejoined Billos, shaking her head. No ball.

Thomas studied his fledgling Guard recruits. "I still don't think any of you are using enough of the muscle between your ears to be counted as leaders. The objective of this entire game was a simple one. You started well, Billos, but have still failed at the objective. Which is what?"

Billos, the seventeen-year-old with dark hair, returned Thomas Hunter's stare. "To cross the opponent's goal with the ball."

"Rules?"

"No killing or intentionally maiming," Billos said.

"Yet the ball has yet to cross the line. You have all failed to satisfy this objective." Thomas walked around them, swinging his sword angrily. "You've all stood here like idiots engaging me. The opportunities for victory have been countless in these last few minutes!"

Silence.

"I do think I could take any sixteen-year-old from the crowd and show them stronger than any of you."

"Then do it!" Jackov screamed.

Thomas swung to him. "There are no rules in matters of wit and mind, Jackov, but I still haven't made my final selection. You should watch your emotion."

Jackov saw his mistake and bowed his head. "Forgive me."

"I will. And I will agree to your insistence that I . . . *do it*."

He faced Johnis. "You there, who stepped out first. What is your name?"

At first Johnis wasn't sure he was speaking to him, but there could be no mistake. All eyes were on him.

"Johnis," he said.

"Johnis. How old are you?"

"Sixteen."

"Are you married, Johnis?"

"No," Johnis said.

"Well then, I think we have our new player." Thomas faced his fighters. "I do think that this boy, who was either too cowardly to try out for the Guard or was dismissed early, could run circles around the lot of you."

Jackov spit to one side.

Rather than consider his options in slow deliberation, Johnis once again reacted on impulse, trusting his heart. He simply did what he knew he must do if he wanted to avoid a terrible end to this day.

"Should I invite him to show you all a lesson?" Thomas demanded of his fighters.

Without any further invitation, Johnis left his spot by the side and walked toward Jackov.

Quick thinking.

Deadly thinking.

FIVE

J ohnis was halfway across the field before he'd fully decided on what he would do. He'd committed himself to either being beaten to a pulp, as Thomas had put it, or teaching them all that a smaller boy with a love for books wasn't as useless as they thought.

A slight grin settled on Thomas Hunter's face. "You've come out for your whipping so eagerly, lad?"

"No, sir," Johnis said, striding faster now. Straight for Jackov. "I've come out to show the big thug that mind is greater than muscle." He wasn't entirely sure where all of this courage was coming from.

Courage or stupidity?

Jackov grunted and took a step in Johnis's direction.

At this point Johnis could do one of two things. He could continue on—into the jaws of this monster, so to speak—or he could turn tail and sprint for the end with the ball safely around his belly.

He supposed that Thomas wanted him to do the latter, to show them all that mind was greater than muscle. But Johnis suddenly wanted to do more.

So he started to jog, arms pumping loosely, hoping that the Horde hair around his waist would stay put.

There were twenty-four fighters on the field, grouped at the center. There were five thousand onlookers in the stadium. There was one supreme commander, Thomas Hunter, standing to one side.

And every last eyeball was pinned to him. To Johnis. Heading straight into terrible trouble.

"I want you to put this cheeky lad on the ground, Jackov," Thomas growled in a low voice heard by all on the field. "Don't maim or kill him, but I want you to hurt him."

Jackov needed no encouragement. He was moving forward already.

So then, perhaps Johnis's plan wasn't quite so smart after all. Why had Thomas Hunter turned against him? The Horde had killed his mother, the Forest Guard had dismissed him from service, and now the supreme commander himself, leader of all the forests, had ordered the strongest young fighter to beat him to a pulp.

Why?

Johnis set the question aside and breathed deeply. They were twenty yards from a head-on collision when he suddenly pulled up and slid to a stop.

Johnis reached under his shirt, grabbed one end of the Horde hair, and yanked it free. It hung from his hand like a knotted whip.

Those in the crowd who didn't know he had the football gasped. Jackov blinked. He missed a step. They were no more than ten feet apart.

"My mother paid for this Horde hair with her life," Johnis screamed. "Now it's yours!"

He flung the cords of hair high in the air, toward Jackov. The larger boy shifted his attention from Johnis to the ball.

Johnis launched himself up and into Jackov then. His years of running had made him fast, and he was light. His body left the ground like a battering ram, fists forward.

But he didn't strike the other fighter with his fists. One measly blow with his knuckles would do nothing but daze Jackov. Instead, he jerked his arms wide at the last moment, pulling apart Jackov's hands to make way for his flying body.

Johnis felt the top of his head thud squarely against Jackov's unprotected face.

Pain flashed down his spine, then was gone. Johnis landed hard, rolled to his feet, and spun back. The Horde hair was still airborne, sailing straight toward him.

Jackov, on the other hand, was on both knees, shaking the cobwebs out of his head.

Johnis snatched the Horde hair from the air and stood in a

crouch, feeling confident and ready for a counter. But he decided quickly that another attack wouldn't go nearly so smoothly for him, so he made a show of bravado by spinning to face Thomas.

"Is that what you had in mind?" he demanded.

The supreme commander had lost his smile. He stared hard, and Johnis wasn't sure what to make of that. Hadn't he done well?

Without waiting for Jackov to fully recover, Johnis turned his back on the group of stunned fighters, jogged to the end zone, dropped the Horde hair football unceremoniously on the ground, and faced the stadium.

For a moment the silence was so thick Johnis wondered if he was in a dream. Jackov was standing beside the other fighters, looking at him.

Darsal was grinning, but Johnis couldn't tell if it was a wicked grin or one of satisfaction.

Silvie frowned, her jaw muscles bunched.

Billos had crossed his arms and was pretending to be interested in something in the trees. A company of parrots squawked and took flight over the stadium. Okay, so maybe he had seen something.

Milic, a friend to Johnis, was the only fighter on the field who was clearly pleased with this turn of events.

Johnis started to walk for the sidelines, unsure how he was supposed to feel. Or what he was supposed to do, for that matter. He wasn't even sure what had happened.

His father suddenly thrust both fists above his head and

screamed his approval in a terrifying, raspy wail. Cheering erupted like a huge wave, thundering cries of approval.

Johnis stopped. For the first time the significance of his feat became clear. He might not be eligible for the Forest Guard—in all honesty he wasn't even sure he *wanted* to be eligible. But in his mind he'd honored the memory of his mother, Rosa, by crossing the line for all to see, with the very Horde hair harvested by his father.

He'd followed his instincts, and he'd done it for love of his mother. He had thought with his heart, as Thomas himself had insisted the others do.

Thomas Hunter strode toward him, face sullen. He stopped and took a bow. "Well done, lad."

He stepped forward and touched the top of Johnis's head, the tips of his fingers bloody as he retracted his hand. He gripped Johnis's jaw and turned his head gently as if examining him for something, then lowered his arm. "You have won the horse that I was going to give to Jackov." Thomas bowed again. "Thank you. You may join your father."

Johnis walked off the field to another roar from the crowd, still unsure how he felt about all of this.

His father dipped his head. "Elyon's strength, boy."

"Elyon's strength."

Thomas raised his hand at the center of the field and the throng quieted.

"I've made my decision," the supreme commander said, pacing

around the group of fighters. "These are dangerous times we live in. We have received word from our scouts that the Horde is gathering to the east"—he pointed his sword toward his left, east-ward—"and will march on this forest in four days with an army over two hundred thousand strong."

Johnis caught his breath. Such a large army against their much smaller Guard? A parrot squawked far away.

"Normally our recruits would prepare for months before being thrust into battle, but those days are gone," Thomas said. "The thousand new recruits will fight by our sides in four days' time."

A mother cried out. But only one. Somewhere a child was crying, oblivious to all.

Four days. It was too soon for sixteen- and seventeen-year-old fighters! They would be slaughtered. True, on a good day one guardsman could handle ten Scabs, but these new recruits would be lucky to handle one.

This was grave news indeed. Johnis felt a terrible pity for the twenty-four young fighters on the field, not to mention the other 976 pups who would rush out to face the Horde in four days.

Thomas continued. "I know they are young, but they are strong. We have no choice. The ten-thousand-member Guard we now have in this forest needs every advantage."

The somberness of his decision to throw the young recruits into battle so soon began to sink in. Johnis felt a knot rise in his throat.

"I need four strong leaders under my seasoned commanders,

and today I have found them," Thomas said. "As agreed, each will be given a house, a choice of horse, and an emerald-handled sword. In addition, as soon as they have finished one final test this very day, each will be promoted to the rank of lieutenant."

Johnis watched the four who would receive the honor. He couldn't quite imagine Darsal or Billos, or even Jackov, swinging a sword into the chests of the beasts called the Horde. They'd be shredded like taro root.

Thomas faced the recruits. "Take a knee, all of you."

They all knelt.

"If you are willing to give your life for the forests and for Elyon, and to lead others to that same end, stand and step forward as I speak your name."

As was customary for special selection, the twenty-four fighters lowered their heads.

Thomas pointed his sword at the witty, dark-haired boy with high cheekbones who was well known as Billos. "Billos of the Southern Forest, step forward if you will."

Billos rose, stepped forward, and kissed Thomas's sword, signifying his acceptance to die if his service required it. The silence was thick.

Thomas pointed to Silvie, the spicy blond with brilliant eyes and as-of-yet unscarred skin. "Silvie of Northern, step forward if you will."

She rose, kissed the sword, and took her place next to Billos.

"Darsal of the Southern Forest, step forward if you will."

She did.

Still no cheering. The moment was too sacred, for this was a moment in which each was choosing to die as much as live.

Thomas pointed his sword at Jackov of the Northern Forest. Johnis felt gratitude flood his chest. It had been one thing to beat Jackov in the game, but he didn't want the boy to miss such an opportunity on account of him.

He sighed softly and lowered his head. For the first time since he dumped the Horde football in the end zone, Johnis smiled. The day had turned out well.

"And for the fourth I choose you," Thomas's voice rang out. "Step forward if you will."

Johnis wasn't watching. He was thinking of that one final test Thomas had said these four must face. Customarily it would be a task that would force the new leaders to work as a team. More than once a chosen leader had failed the final test and been sent back to the squad to be replaced.

"Are you refusing my commission?" Thomas asked.

What was this? Johnis lifted his head, wondering what had gotten into Jackov to refuse the commission. But he didn't see Jackov refusing the commission.

He saw Thomas pointing his sword in his direction.

At *him*.

Johnis's heart stopped. A shiver passed down his neck.

Him?

But that was impossible. He didn't want to be the *him* this sword was pointing at. Didn't want to go out battling the Horde in four days' time. Didn't want a new house or a new horse.

In fact, staring at Thomas's sword, Johnis was terrified to be counted as one of the Forest Guard, much less lead a swarm of fighters into bloody battle.

It occurred to him that everyone was silent. Waiting for him.

"I can't," he said.

"You can't? Or you won't?" Thomas said, sword unwavering.

"I was dismissed," Johnis said.

"Consider yourself *un*dismissed."

"I'm too young."

"Have you ever given your heart to a woman?" Thomas asked. He hesitated. "Yes."

"Then you're old enough to fight for love and for the Great Romance," the commander said, speaking of their religion, which revolved around love.

"I'm too small," Johnis said. "I'm a lover, not a fighter."

Thomas angrily thrust his sword into the dirt. "Any lover of Elyon or any of his creatures is a fighter for Elyon and his creatures! I will decide if you are too young or too small or too slow or too cheeky for your own good! Do you understand?"

"Yes."

"And I have decided that you are more worthy than all of these!" Thomas pointed to the fighters he'd rejected as leaders. "Are you questioning my judgment? I, who have crossed the worlds, who have hung my life out to be swatted at by the Horde in every battle since the blasted Shataiki ravaged the land! You think your fresh little mind can match my judgment?"

"No, sir."

A woman stepped out from the bleachers on Johnis's left. Rachelle, wife to Thomas, wore a short fighting tunic and leather sandals with straps that crisscrossed up her calves to her knees. A knife was secured to her thigh.

Legend had it that Rachelle had taught Thomas everything he knew of fighting—and of love—when he'd fallen into this world from another long before the Great Deception. Watching her slink toward him, Johnis thought the legends had to be right.

She seemed to rob the breath from even Thomas.

Rachelle stepped up to Johnis and studied him, smiling gently. She took his chin in her hand and turned his face, as Thomas had done.

"He's right, you know," she said. "You're a born leader. The world will turn on you. You are chosen."

Johnis was about to step forward and accept when she continued.

"You do realize that the girls will fall in line to marry you now, don't you?" She winked. "I recommend you trust my husband. Everything he's done, he's done for your good. There is no one I know who has better judgment than Thomas."

Johnis felt short of breath. He stepped forward on legs that felt not entirely there.

"Will you?" Thomas asked again.

Johnis walked out to the supreme leader, kissed the handle of the sword that still jutted from the earth, and bowed. "I will."

Again it was Johnis's father who cried out first, but this time with a hoarse voice from all of his yelling earlier. Five thousand strong stood to their feet and roared at the sky, then began to stomp the earth so that it shook.

Thomas let them roar for a full minute, while Johnis stood quietly, head bowed, unsure of what they expected from him or what the other three thought of him.

When the cheers quieted, he lifted his head and saw that Thomas had raised his sword. Eyes on him.

"To receive your commission, you will arm yourselves and ride on four of our fastest horses directly west to the Igal point. There you will retrieve a group of four marked catalina cacti at the forest's edge and return them by nightfall without breaking a single needle."

"Four?" Billos said. "They're too large."

Thomas shot him a glare. "That, lad, is the point. You'll have to use your heads and work as a team."

"What about the Horde?" Johnis asked.

"Well, you can't very well love them to death, can you, Johnis?" Thomas grinned. "I wouldn't be too concerned—our reports have them to the east. You're headed west, young man. If you're lucky enough to run into a straggler or two, bring me more hair for my football."

The fighters chuckled, but Johnis found no reason to join them.

"The sun is sinking. I suggest you get your bruised bodies to

the stables and fly like the wind. It's a two-hour ride from here."
Thomas spread his arms and turned in a circle, addressing the
crowd. "Send them off, lovers of Elyon. Tell them they will not
give their lives in vain!"

And they did, though Johnis couldn't actually understand the
jumbled cries of encouragement beating against his ears.

No one noticed the hooded man slipping discreetly from the
stadium's southern entrance. He hurried into the forest, mounted a
black steed that was awaiting him, and pounded into the shadows.

Toward the desert.

Toward the Horde.

SIX

Seen from high above, Johnis's world was mostly pale desert sand. No oceans, no islands, no continents. Canyons and valleys were filled with sand and rock, not trees or ponds.

But if one looked closely, he would find seven forests, each roughly a day's walk across. And at the center of each forest, a green lake. And around each lake, a large village inhabited by the Forest Dwellers. Each forest was simply designated by its position relative to the Middle Forest. Thomas's Forest.

The Middle Forest village—which was more of a city than a village, judging by size alone—was built in large circles with the lake at the center, the lake that contained the powerful cleansing waters they all depended on for their health. Flowering vines blossomed on most of the wood houses—a garden splashed in reds and blues and yellows.

Bathing in the lake once each day kept the Forest Dwellers' skin free of the painful, scaly disease that turned the Horde gray. Miss a day of bathing and the pain would begin at the joints, spreading outward.

Miss two days and the skin would begin to crack.

Miss three days and you were pretty much a Scab, one of the Horde, covered from head to foot in the flaking disease. Worse, your mind would succumb to the delusion the Horde had regarding the dangers of water.

The lake, first found by Thomas Hunter, was Elyon's gift to them, an escape from the evil that had latched itself onto the Scabs. Each evening the village celebrated the Great Romance at the lake's shores at what was called the Gathering. There they danced and sang of Elyon's love, retelling the legends of a time only thirteen years earlier when they could breathe the intoxicating waters and laugh with Elyon himself if they so desired.

According to the legends, before the disease had come, large white bats with furry bodies—known as Roush—had guarded their paradise. Back then, the evil black Shataiki vampire bats were confined to the Black Forest, behind a green river they could not cross.

But the river had been crossed by a human, and the Shataiki had been set free to ravage the land. The evil once confined to the Black Forest now clung to the skin and minds of all who refused to follow the single escape that Elyon had left them all. Seven lakes in seven forests.

This all according to legend, of course.

But since that day, not one Roush had been seen. Not a single Shataiki vampire bat. Well over a million Horde now waged war on a hundred thousand followers of Elyon. Because of legend.

Indeed, although they bathed daily and defended their way of life against the Horde, most Forest Dwellers at least questioned the truth of the legends (although it had been only thirteen years). Had there ever really been a magical lake whose waters you could breathe? Did Roush and Shataiki bats ever really roam the land? Had Teeleh actually brought the disease on the Horde? For that matter, did the lakes really come from some unknown god called Elyon?

Or were all of these simply religious explanations to describe a natural disease that was healed by the medicines contained in the lakes? Only thirteen years had passed since the whole planet had been ravaged by the disease, true, but who was to say that these memories had not been caused by the disease itself? There was no real evidence to the contrary today.

Eager to complete their final quest before the day was gone, Billos, Darsal, Silvie, and Johnis prepared for the journey in the same way all Forest Guard did before undertaking any mission: they equipped themselves with leather battle-dress, thin horns to blow to warn of danger, knives, and their new emerald-handled swords. They'd loaded enough bathing water and food for two days—those were the requirements.

Johnis was assigned the task of gathering food. With help from his father and younger sister, he grabbed what he could from their kitchen: taro root and some soft sago cakes, both good for starch. Fruit, of course. Nanka, blingblings, rhambutan.

"You want the plum pudding?" Kiella asked. "I'll put it in a shoe so it won't smoosh."

"Now, what would I do with plum pudding?" Johnis demanded, feeling both frustrated and admittedly a little proud that he had been selected. "You think the Forest Guard takes desserts with them when they fight the Scabs?"

"I would," she said. "It'll keep you sweet."

"That'll just make me better for the Horde to eat," he said, knowing the Horde didn't really eat human flesh.

Kiella's eyes went wide, and she said nothing more.

"Hurry, lad," his father urged, bursting into the kitchen, face bright with pride. "They've gathered to send you off!" He waved him forward with a thick, gnarled hand. "Come, hurry, come!"

Johnis got his finer frame and features from his mother, she'd always told him: His pronounced cheekbones and dark hair. His brown eyes, too often covered by bangs for her liking. His fingers, better for the pen than for the sword, his father had once said. Mother disagreed. He was perfect for both!

Johnis loved his father, but he'd cherished his mother, Rosa, with every living fiber.

Johnis met the other three new leaders at the square fifteen minutes later and galloped out of the village with Thomas's last words ringing in his ears.

"Think with your hearts. Elyon's strength!"

JOHNIS RODE AT THE REAR OF THE PARTY, JUST BEHIND Silvie. For the first hour not a word was spoken.

The entire business was wrong, he thought. Completely and absurdly wrong! He'd stumbled along behind the others, out of the stadium, into the lake, into the battle-dress, dumbly doing what was expected of him.

You're in the Forest Guard now, Johnis!

His childhood fantasy of slaying the Horde at the end of the wooden sword his father had given him when he'd turned three had been laced with glory, not this vow to lead others into death. And in four days' time! A Horde army of several hundred thousand strong would leave plenty of dead under hoof.

The muscles of the huge black steed under him rippled, sweaty. If they kept up this pace, they would kill their horses. Ahead, Silvie's short, wavy hair rose and fell. It occurred to him that he had no clue who these three people were apart from the bits he'd heard. They hadn't even spoken to him since leaving the stadium.

Darsal and Billos both came from the Southern Forest, and they shared an uncommon bond that came from years of knowing secrets, he thought. All he knew about Darsal was that her father had died in battle when she was young.

Billos, who had been so talkative on the field, led them in stern silence. He rode as if the mission was his alone to finish.

They all did.

Johnis reined in his horse and came to a stomping halt. The other three galloped on without a glance backward, uncaring. They disappeared through the trees. Any lingering hope that they might include him vanished. He was alone and—

A *screech* from the trees cut his self-pity short. Johnis jerked his head and scanned the branches, but nothing looked out of the ordinary. No parrots or possums that he could see. Only leafy green branches swaying in the wind.

Eeeaaaak!

Johnis shifted his sight to his right. A shadow perched at the top of a mango tree.

A shadow with red eyes.

A shadow with red eyes and large black wings that now spread slowly to a span of three feet.

Johnis caught his breath. The bird or bat or whatever this beast was stared at him for several long seconds, then leaped straight up, leaving nothing but rustling leaves behind.

He'd heard a thousand stories of the Shataiki beasts, and in his mind's eye they had always looked exactly like that. But that was impossible. No one had seen a Shataiki since the Great Deception.

Johnis kicked his horse hard. It bolted forward and galloped full tilt through the trees. In the space of ten breaths he'd caught the others.

"Stop!"

They ignored him and sped on.

"Stop, I said!" he yelled, angry now.

Billos pulled up hard, spun his horse around, and kneed past Johnis. "Shut your flap, boy!" he rasped. "Every Scab in ten miles will hear you. You want us all dead?"

Darsal and Silvie had come to a stop twenty yards farther and were staring back without expression. Johnis had intended to tell them about the Shataiki, but he knew immediately by Billos's tone of voice and the looks on their faces that they would only scoff. He switched tactics.

"No, I don't want us dead, which is why I suggest we stop running the horses," Johnis said. "We'll kill them, and without horses we *could* be dead."

Billos's mount snorted heavily, flesh quivering. Sweat wet its shoulders and rump.

"Was I born yesterday?" Billos demanded. "I'd take a dead horse over a Horde scouting party any day."

"I don't know; I think you could handle a few Scabs pretty easily," Johnis said, in an attempt to win some favor back.

Billos jerked his new sword free of its scabbard and whipped its blade up to Johnis's neck. The boy was fast. Very fast.

"You're right," Billos said. "But that's *my* call, not yours."

"Then what's your call? Do we walk the horses, or do we ride them to death?"

Billos hesitated.

"Watch your cheek, boy," Darsal said sternly, walking her horse back. "That may have been a cute trick you played in the stadium, but you have no right to fight by my side. You aren't a true soldier. If you want to live long enough to marry, you should turn back now. Give it up."

She is beautiful despite the terrible scar, Johnis thought. *And cruel.* Separating Darsal and Billos would be like separating the ironwood bark from its tree.

"You're suggesting that I defy Thomas," Johnis said. "Believe me, this wasn't my idea."

"You're a reject," Billos said. "There's not enough muscle on you to swing a sword, much less kill a Scab."

"Tell that to Jackov," Johnis said. "Tell it to the supreme commander. But for now, make your call. Do we run the horses or walk them?"

Three sets of eyes drilled him. If Johnis wasn't mistaken, Silvie didn't share Billos and Darsal's hatred of him. But he wasn't sure. She sat small on the huge mount, looking back at him with lost blue eyes and that flawless tanned face. He held her gaze there. Intelligent, they said, but how intelligent?

Darsal grunted and jerked her horse around.

"We should walk our mounts," Silvie said.

Billos gave Johnis a parting glare, trotted to the front, and slowed his horse to a walk. "We walk."

A shriek pierced the air to the west. Johnis looked to the sky and nudged his horse forward, thoughts of their cruelty suddenly gone.

No sign of the black bat. But now the same far cry came from his left, above the trees. A flight of black flickered through the branches.

They passed into a clearing, and Johnis pulled up right next to Silvie. He scanned the perimeter for bats. No flying beasts that he could see, but they rustled through the treetops on both sides now.

He spun his head to Silvie and saw that she was studying him with that same soft look that seemed frozen on her face.

"Did you hear that?" Johnis asked.

She just stared at him. Obviously not.

"None of you can hear that?"

"Shut your flap, Scrapper," Billos snapped without turning.

They walked on. The horses' hooves clumped softly. The trees rustled.

The sky shrieked softly on both sides.

Johnis shivered. Something very wrong was happening, and he seemed to be the only one who knew or cared.

"What do you hear?" Silvie asked.

Johnis wasn't sure she could handle the truth. He gave it to her anyway. "We're being followed by Shataiki bats on both sides. They're crying out. You don't hear them?"

"We hear your fear," Billos said, looking at him. "The Shataiki are the stuff of legends; they don't exist. Evil is everywhere you look and wears the face of a Scab, not some ghost in the sky. Everyone knows that."

No one disagreed.

"You do realize that you and I will be leading campaigns together one day," Johnis said. "We should work together, but you're so bitter about nothing that you're exposing your flank to the vilest creatures at this very moment. Thomas would be proud."

"He's exposing his flank to a ghost," Darsal answered. "Look, maybe we will lead campaigns together if we survive the month. Only Elyon knows. But our objective today is to retrieve the cacti and return them to the village in one piece. That would have been much easier if Jackov were sitting on that horse instead of you. Do you disagree?"

She had a point. "You may be right. But if you do want to return to the village in one piece, you'd better at least listen. They're following us this very minute."

As if to agree, a long cry cut through the air on their right. Johnis spun and pointed. "There!"

The black bat rose from the treetops slowly, banked, and soared overhead, pupilless eyes staring down like two shiny red tomatoes.

Eeeaaaak . . .

"There, you see it, right above? Don't tell me you can't see it!"

They all looked up. "No, we can't see it," Silvie said. "And if you want us to take you seriously, I suggest you set this nonsense aside."

Johnis decided he had no alternative but to bide his time. His eyes were not fooling him—he knew that much. Something was very wrong—he knew that as well. But for the moment he could only follow these insolent thugs.

"I heard about your mother," Silvie said, casting him that same frozen look. "The Horde ball. Losing someone so close can do terrible things to a person."

"I appreciate your concern," Johnis said.

"I don't mean it in a cruel way. It's just that my father and mother were both killed by the Horde. I understand how it feels. I left a life of study, destined for the priesthood, on account of it."

Johnis felt a pang of empathy for her. The brightest from each forest were selected for special training to teach others the ways of life. Science, arts, religion, history—everything but war. She'd taken up fighting only after her parents were killed.

"How did it happen?"

"My mother was taken in battle four years ago," Silvie said. "My father went after her and they killed him as well. Now they'll take me, but not before I take a hundred of them."

"Only four years? You look like you were born with a knife in your hand."

She looked at him, unsure.

"I mean that in a good way, of course," Johnis said. "You learn fast."

She shrugged. "Be the best at what you do, my father used to say. Billos lost his mother and Darsal her father. Both to the Horde. In this way we're all the same."

"Losing someone to the Horde doesn't make you worthy to lead," Billos said.

Darsal's jaw flexed. "What good is a father if he's off to war his whole life?"

"I'm sorry you feel no respect for the dead," Silvie said. "But I do."

Darsal spit to one side. *There is indeed a story here,* Johnis thought. Darsal drew her motivation from hate, Silvie from revenge. Either way, they were finally talking, and for that Johnis was grateful.

They were halfway across the large clearing and the shrieks on each side now came from dozens of Shataiki, assuming that's what they really were. For this, Johnis was far less grateful.

But he couldn't return to the subject, not yet. He had to prod them with something else if he wanted to keep them talking.

"I realize that my being here is a complete fluke," Johnis said, "and I respect your frustration. I'm a lover and a poet, not a fighter, although I'm better with a sword than you might think. Either way, I want to thank each of you for being selected. I know it means you'll all probably be dead within the month. But you're the best in the forests."

"Shut your yapper, Scrapper," Billos said.

The boy's rudeness was too much for Johnis. "It's comforting to ride with such strong company when you're surrounded by Shataiki, even though you're all too blind to see them. Speaking of which, I really do think—"

"Silence, boy!" Darsal snarled. "I swear, I'll cut your tongue out and shove it so far down your throat you won't need to eat for a month!"

Her voice echoed through the clearing, but the sound was quickly muted by dozens of black bats suddenly taking flight on each side. They screamed and flapped into the sky, spreading wide leathery wings like kites.

It struck Johnis that Darsal wasn't the one they'd reacted to. He stopped his horse and scanned the perimeter. "Silvie! You have to listen to me."

"It's okay, Johnis," she interrupted. "Some people think I'm a little crazy—"

Four beige stallions bred for the desert stepped out of the forest thirty paces ahead. On each sat a Horde, dressed in black leathers known to be worn by the Horde's assassins, Qurong's elite guard. The Scabs were tall and stately despite the rotting skin that fell from their bones.

Johnis smelled them at the same time he saw them. He'd heard thousands of stories, he'd felt the pain they brought, he'd even seen a dead Scab or two, but this was the first time he had seen a Horde warrior face-to-face.

These four had come for a purpose.

They'd come to kill the young.

SEVEN

For a long moment the four new recruits stood frozen like desert rocks. A hundred thoughts flew through their minds. Johnis was aware only of his own.

I'm too young to die.

This is all a mistake; I'm too young to die.

Then his impulsiveness took over. Even as the other three slipped their swords from their leather scabbards without so much as budging their horses, Johnis kicked his mount hard and bolted to the right at a full gallop, to the edge of the clearing.

He was running. He was tucking tail and fleeing in terror.

Or so he desperately hoped the Scabs would think.

From the corner of his eye, he saw two of them break off and thunder after him, leaving two to fight Billos, Darsal, and Silvie. Three against two. That was a good thing.

Then again, there were now two Scabs pounding down his one backside. This was a bad thing.

Johnis had just passed into the trees when he heard the first cries of battle from behind. Billos and Darsal as one, screaming in rage as they took swords either from or to the elite Horde fighters. Silvie would fight in silence, he guessed. It was her way.

Now Johnis had two options: He could turn and fight—his younger, inexperienced body swinging his as-yet-undrawn sword against two older, battle-hardened beasts. An absurd proposition to say the least.

Or he could dance his way around these trees, hoping one or both of the Scabs would collide with a branch and be knocked silly so that he could then dismount and behead them before they woke.

An even more absurd proposition.

Fighting was out of the question, he decided. He wasn't here to kill Scabs. He was here to retrieve the catalina cacti with the others, return to the village, and then explain to Thomas Hunter that he'd made a dreadful mistake. When Johnis had said "I will" in the stadium, he'd really meant "I won't," but the beauty of Thomas's wife, Rachelle, had messed with his thinking.

Johnis ducked his way around trees and caught sight of the two black wraiths hounding him like shadows. They rode in silence, but their horses pounded and snorted. He could practically feel the hot air from their nostrils blasting against his neck.

Forest Guard horses were said to be faster than the Horde's, but the tight trees took away this advantage. They were actually gaining!

Johnis veered to his right, cutting back toward the clearing. He had to get back into the open to give his horse a chance. And if he couldn't break away, he would draw his sword and try to kill at least one before they chopped him.

But there was a chance that his very first instinct would prove right. In which case he wouldn't run *or* turn and fight. He would lead these two beasts into a trap.

He galloped free of the trees several hundred yards down from where he'd first entered them. To his far right, three horses stood where there should have been five.

Two had fled. The two desert horses were gone.

Billos, Darsal, and Silvie sat on their stamping mounts, swords still drawn.

Johnis jerked his horse right and thundered toward them. Behind him the two dense thugs followed. Hope swelled in his chest.

He was fewer than fifty yards from the other three when one of the horses in pursuit whinnied. He glanced back and saw that the Scabs had smelled the trap and were reining back.

"Go!" Johnis yelled. "Go, go!"

Billos, Darsal, and Silvie went. They flew past Johnis, headed straight toward the two stunned Scabs behind him, who by now had surely seen their fallen comrades in heaps on the grass, dead.

Johnis turned his mount and kneed him forward. But the

three new Forest Guard fighters didn't appear to need his help. Darsal and Billos split wide left and right, forcing the two Scabs to cover their flanks while Silvie drove straight up the middle toward them.

Johnis watched in fascination as the battle unfolded like a choreographed dance. Even though the three recruits had been in training only two weeks, they worked together flawlessly.

Seeing Silvie bearing down on them, the Scabs both shifted their attention to her. She dropped her sword and whipped out a knife.

At the same moment Billos screamed, bearing down from the right, and Darsal from the left. For a split moment, both Scabs diverted their attention to the two fighters at their sides.

Silvie threw her knife. And then a second knife Johnis hadn't seen her draw. But she hadn't thrown the knives at the Scabs. Rather at their horses, much larger targets.

The blades glanced off the strong shoulder of one horse and clipped the side of the other, enough to make both jerk and snort in pain.

Billos and Darsal swung their swords when the Scabs were off balance.

For the first time, Johnis watched diseased Scabs fall in battle. And it was a gruesome sight. The earth shook when they landed. Then they lay still, and their horses bolted into the forest.

A lone Shataiki screeched and took flight, soaring away over the canopy toward the west.

Quiet settled on the field. Billos walked his horse back to where Johnis waited in his saddle.

"So you are a coward," he said.

Johnis said nothing. He'd risked his neck to give them a chance.

"You do that again, boy, and I'll help the Horde chase you down," Darsal said.

"It was us four against those four," Johnis said. "I made it you three against two."

Billos scoffed.

"And when you three killed the first two, I led the other two into the same fate," Johnis continued.

"In my mind you are no Guard at all," Billos said, biting off the words. "I will never fight by your side."

"Easy, Billos," Silvie said, kicking her horse into a trot. "Coward or not, we're alive and the Horde are dead." She loped past them toward the west. "We have a mission, and the sun isn't standing still."

"They were waiting for us," Johnis pointed out. "Doesn't that bother you?"

"The mind of a coward always sees the worst," Billos snapped. He slapped his horse and brushed past Johnis.

It took them another half hour to reach the Igal point at the forest's edge. Johnis once again rode at the rear. The Shataiki began showing up after ten minutes, but apart from their red stares and wicked cries they made no attempt to stop the fighters, so Johnis avoided another verbal lashing by keeping this observation to himself.

Still, two thoughts beat through his mind. First, he alone saw the bats, which he guessed had always been there, unseen by the Forest Dwellers. And second, they probably *were* being led into a trap. But he was powerless to change their course.

Darsal was leading when they reached the last line of trees, and she lifted her hand to stop them. They pulled up beside her, four abreast.

Beyond the tree trunks lay the canyons with their flat shale tops that fell away to the desert sands. And beyond the canyons, sand dunes as far as the eye could see. The sun was already halfway down to the horizon. Soon the sky would turn bloodred, as it did every evening.

"Do you see anything?" Billos asked.

They scanned the desert for sign of Scabs. And cacti. Just beyond the forest a tall rock jutted fifty yards into the sky. This was the Igal point. Climb its peak and they said you could see for a day's ride.

"Should we scale the point?" Darsal asked no one in particular.

"We don't have time," Silvie said. "Do you see the cacti?"

Billos guided his horse out of the trees and stopped for them to join him.

"Do you see it?" Darsal asked again.

"There's no clump of four that I can see. That one to the left there is small and by itself. Maybe he meant for us to find four separate ones."

"No, he said a group of four," Johnis said, coaxing his ride to the right where the rock shelf hung over a ravine.

"But there's no saying what he meant by 'group,'" Billos persisted.

"Even so, I don't see four," Silvie said. "The catalina cactus likes sand. We'd have to go deeper into these canyons to find more."

"Either way, I think two of us should make the stretcher we'll need to carry them back unharmed," Darsal said. They'd already decided to return the large cacti home safely by strapping them to two long poles with branches between to form a stretcher.

"Fine," Billos said, "the coward could manage that task, I would think."

But Johnis hardly heard him, because he'd come to the edge of the ravine and could now see that they were in more than a little bit of trouble. The shelf fell off ten feet to a bed of sand that stretched into a widening canyon.

Their catalina cacti were at the base of this shelf, growing from the sandy bottom. He'd found them, and that was good.

But so had someone else.

Found them and smashed them to bits.

"I found them," Johnis said.

"Where?" They hurried over and stared into the ravine with him.

Each cactus had to have been as tall as a horse, judging by the size of the green chunks that littered the floor. For a moment they were all too stunned to speak.

"Elyon help us!"

"Now what?" Johnis said.

Billos forced his horse in a tight circle, studying the terrain.

"You know now what," he said. "We have no choice. There have to be four more, deeper in."

Silvie studied the desert. "Deeper? Do you think that's wise?"

"What choice do we have?"

"Ride along the forest edge," she said.

"The large ones don't grow in rocks!" Darsal said. "Billos is right: we have to go deeper where we know they are, or we could spend hours looking for nothing."

Johnis took his eyes off the shattered cacti and looked farther into the canyon. Didn't these recruits, the best of all the young fighters, see what was so obvious to him? The Horde had done this. It was a trap!

Johnis turned back, thinking how he should drop this little jewel into their minds, when movement at the treetops stopped him cold.

He hadn't noticed them because they weren't squawking, but the Shataiki had come. By the hundreds. Even more—too many to count, perched on the branches, staring at them with their beady eyes.

His horse shifted and snorted, as if it, too, had noticed.

Silvie followed his stare, then looked into his eyes, searching him.

Johnis spoke quietly for her to hear. "The Horde know we're here. They obviously smashed the plants and are waiting for us to enter the canyons. Surely you can see that."

"Of course the Horde smashed them," Silvie said. "They eat the smelly flesh at the center. That doesn't mean it's a trap."

"The coward is seeing ghosts again." Billos smirked. "I suppose the Shataiki are swarming the trees again—isn't that right, Scrapper?"

"The Horde were waiting for us in the clearing, and if we head into the desert they'll be waiting for us again," Johnis insisted. "We know the Horde is gathering. This doesn't seem to be the time to go into the desert alone."

Billos blew some air and rolled his eyes. "Please. The Horde is on the other side of the forest, in the east. We're on the western side. Does logic escape you completely?"

Johnis studied the canyons, not sure how he felt any longer. It wasn't fear that cautioned him. It was, in fact, common sense.

"We have a mission," Billos snapped, growing impatient. "Are you refusing to come?"

"No. I'm just telling you what I know."

"Save your knowledge for children, poet. We're wasting time."

Billos nudged his horse to the edge, then slapped it hard. It plunged over the lip, rode a small landslide of tumbling stones, and landed by the cacti far below.

One by one they followed his lead. The moment they headed down the canyon, the Shataiki bats left the trees and lined the cliff edges on either side of them. A foul stench drifted into the stuffy ravine, smothering Johnis.

He'd bided his time with these fools, but now his patience was growing thin. Even his younger sister, Kiella, wouldn't have had any trouble believing that if you added everything up, it amounted to a hellish mess. The fires were reaching up and licking at their backsides. That was the advantage of a young mind—believing was easier.

Perhaps that was part of this "thinking with your heart" business that Thomas seemed so taken by. Either way, they were headed toward trouble. He could see it, smell it, even feel it.

But instead of trouble, they found large cacti. Two of them. Near the mouth of a deep canyon that branched off to the right a hundred yards from where they'd started.

"There!" Billos pulled out his sword, swung his leg over the saddle, and dropped to the ground. "What did I say?"

An obvious question ran through Johnis's mind. "How do we carry them out?"

Billos cocked his sword back and jerked his head toward Johnis. "You're still with us? I thought I ordered you to cut the saplings for a stretcher."

"I—"

"Hightail it, Scrapper. We're not playing ghost any longer."

Silvie turned her horse around. "I'll go with him."

Johnis ignored Billos's insults and headed back out of the deep canyon with Silvie. Behind them, Billos began to hack at the base of the cactus.

"Don't listen to him," Silvie said.

"I'm not."

She nodded. "But Billos is right. The Horde couldn't have

known we were coming to the Igal point. And even if they did, we have no choice. We have our mission."

"My mother had her mission as well," he said. "I had a fever, and she came to the desert for the healing power of this same cactus. Mistakes in the desert kill people, mission or no mission."

That gave her pause. "Point taken," she said. "And for what it's worth, I don't think you're a coward."

Silvie's horse whinnied nervously as they started the turn into the first ravine. Johnis lifted his eyes and saw why immediately.

The animal had smelled Horde.

Not just one or four, but at least twenty this time, headed down the canyon straight toward them.

"I may not be a coward," Johnis said, "but I think I may be dead. Run!"

EIGHT

R un!" Johnis screamed again, whirling back.

"Run!" Silvie cried in support. She galloped back into the ravine in which Billos and Darsal were cutting the cacti. "There's twenty of them on horses! Mount up and run!"

Johnis held up for a moment, undecided. It did no good for all of them to race down the canyon that Silvie, Billos, and Darsal were now in. Twenty Scabs cut off the ravine that led back up to the forest. That left the ravine straight ahead, which was clear as far as he could see.

He'd risked his neck to divide Horde forces once today and gotten his throat cut by Billos.

So be it.

Johnis sped straight ahead, away from the Horde, away from Billos, Darsal, and Silvie.

Across the canyon floor, without trees to dodge, their steeds were faster than the Scabs' horses, but the canyon would eventually give out, maybe box them in.

A glance behind told him that the party of Scabs had indeed split, half after him, half after the others.

Once again the Shataiki shrieked along the tops of the cliffs.

Once again he'd fled his comrades to split the Horde.

Once again he faced death.

What happened now was beyond his control. The canyon would either give him a way back up to the desert floor or end in a box.

He could hear the thudding of hooves behind him. They didn't seem to be falling behind quickly.

Lover of my soul, save this tiny ant from the beasts. He whispered the common prayer in his mind. Then repeated it.

Elyon, lover of my soul, save this creature from the beasts.

The rock walls on each side rose higher, steeper. A box-end was coming—he could sense it.

Without warning, the cliff on his right suddenly gaped into a second smaller ravine. Johnis veered and thundered in. But he'd gone only fifty yards and turned a slight bend before realizing he'd made a mistake.

This smaller canyon ended here! Large boulders twice the size of his horse were piled at the end, blocking any passage. The walls on both sides were vertical, a hundred feet high. One particularly massive stone towered to his right, fifty feet high, but not high enough to reach the top of the cliff.

Dear Elyon, save this scrapper!

The muted sound of hooves on sand boomed just beyond the bend behind him. For the first time in his life, Johnis withdrew his sword with the intent to kill or be killed.

He spun his horse back and swallowed the fist stuck in his throat.

"You are not forgotten, Mother," he said in a soft shaky voice.

"Psst."

An animal was scurrying behind the huge boulder beside him, but Johnis cared more about the ten animals that were about to tear around the corner.

What would Father do in this situation? He'd always wanted Johnis to join the Guard. Well, he had—for about half a day, before being cut down by the Scabs. It would be the shortest time served in the short history of the Forest Guard.

"Psst. Psssssssst."

Johnis turned to the *psst*. A creature, maybe two or three feet tall, white and furry with bat wings and a cute face, stared at him with green eyes, beckoning him with a spindly finger.

Johnis was so startled that for a moment he forgot about the Horde.

"Hurry, boy!" the fuzzy white bat creature cried. "Are you wanting to be steak?"

"What?"

"This way if you want to live!"

The creature ducked behind the rock. Johnis wheeled his horse and hurried forward. A wide gap led into darkness, hidden from the canyon by the boulder. Large enough for a horse.

Johnis could barely see the furry white body of the bat waddling into the darkness. He held his breath and plunged forward into the crevice.

His head hit the stone ceiling once, but the pain was washed away by a dozen thoughts swirling through his mind. Starting with who this creature ahead of him was.

A Roush. His eyes had been opened to the evil Shataiki, and now he'd met a Roush, those wise protectors spoken about in the legends.

Out in the sunlit canyon behind him, one of the Scabs was swearing in confusion. Would they find the opening?

Then he was through the dark passage into what appeared to be a huge hole in the rock, maybe a hundred yards wide. The bowl he was in had two possible exits that he could see. Blue sky above.

No Shataiki.

The Roush had stopped on the sand, twenty paces out, and was looking at him with an impish grin on its face. A cute, cuddly koala bear-looking thing. White as the clouds.

The air whooshed behind him, and Johnis watched in amazement as a second Roush swooped in with wings spread wide, landed on the sand, and waddled over to the other one, eyeing Johnis as it walked.

They faced him in silence, as if he was an unusual thing that had dropped out of the sky. He supposed he was giving them the same look.

"Well, well, well," the second Roush said in a voice that purred softly. "So it begins."

"Uhhh . . ." was all Johnis managed. He glanced back at the gap through which he'd been rescued. No sign of the Horde.

"Forgive us. It's been thirteen years since any human has seen us. You have to understand that this is quite an ordeal, being seen again by such a noble creature."

"You . . . you can speak," Johnis said.

"And so can you," the Roush said. "My name is Michal. This is Gabil. We've rescued you from death."

And so they had.

"Thank you. Thank you, I just . . ." Johnis wasn't sure what "he just." He was grateful to be alive and stunned into amazement all at once.

"It's okay, lad," Michal said. "We—"

"It's fine, fine by us," the first one, Gabil, interrupted. "I'd be stunned by such a daring rescue myself. And I was quite clever, wasn't I? Pulling you out at the last minute."

"Gabil, please, no need to overdo it," Michal said without looking at his comrade. "As we agreed, I'll carry the conversation."

"Of course."

Michal took a short breath. "We don't have as much time as my friend would like. They'll eventually find a way in."

Michal folded his wings behind his back. "We're here, my friend, because you've been chosen for something special."

"Do you mind stepping down?" Gabil asked. "You're just a bit"—he stretched his wing and spindly fingers up— "tall for my tastes. On the horse, that is."

Johnis dropped to the ground, walked several feet closer, and stopped. "So this isn't a dream," he said. "I mean . . . you're really real. I wasn't killed by the Horde back there and am now in another world, speaking to ghosts."

Gabil laughed and wiggled a little jig, delighted.

"Gabil? We talked about this," Michal warned.

"Sorry. He's just so . . . cute."

"He's a man," Michal said. "Sixteen years old. 'Cute' is the wrong word."

"I'll bet the women line up for a chance to get close to you, don't they?" Gabil asked.

Johnis just stared at him, dumb.

"I knew it!" Gabil thrust his fist in the air and threw back his head. "He's *sooooo* . . . cute!"

"Gabil!"

"Sorry."

The silly Roush pulled his right wing over his face and peeked over it with emerald green eyes. "So sorry," he said in a muffled voice.

"Have you ever noticed the mark behind your right ear?" Michal asked.

Johnis touched his neck. He'd never seen it himself, except dimly reflected in water, but he knew he had a birthmark behind his ear—a circle split with two hash marks like an *X*. "Yes."

"The circle mark," Michael said. "A similar tattoo marked humans' foreheads to show they'd been united with a man or woman before the Great Deception wiped out all such markings through the skin disease. It was the symbol of marriage. But on you it means you've been chosen by Elyon."

"Chosen? Aren't we all?" Johnis was still having a hard time accepting the fact that he was talking to two fuzzy white bats.

"All humans are chosen—yes, of course," Michal said. "But you are special."

Johnis didn't know what to say to that, so he said nothing.

"You are chosen to save the humans, lad," Michal continued. "'A chosen child marked by Elyon will prove his worth and destroy the Dark One.' This was the second prophecy given to Thomas Hunter. He's guarded the secret closely to protect the young from coming under attack from anyone wanting to upset the balance. Something similar happened once in history."

This was all quite ridiculous, of course, but Johnis didn't bother stating the obvious. They all knew the original prophecy: that a way would come when things were at their worst. But this bit about it coming from a boy seemed preposterous to him.

"How's that tied to saving us humans?" he asked.

Gabil pulled his leathery wing from his face and blurted the answer. "By dealing with the slimy, black, flea-infested, snaky, beady-eyed bat vermin one final time, lad!"

"No, actually, that's not it, Gabil," Michal said.

"Or something like that," the shorter Roush insisted. "In the end, anyway."

Michal reached behind him and pulled out a leather-bound book he'd kept hidden until now. Two straps of red twine were wrapped around the ancient black cover—one at the top, one at the bottom—binding it shut. It looked like a small journal.

The Roush held the book out for a moment, then dropped it into the sand, where it landed with a soft thump. "Your task is to find the six lost Books of History."

The book looked magical, sitting still in the sand, staring up at him, halfway between his booted feet and the Roush's thin, bare toes.

"I don't think you understand," Johnis said, searching for something intelligent to say. "I'm actually just a new recruit in the Forest Guard. We're here to take four cacti back to the village. In fact, I should probably get out of here and help my friends."

"Cute," Gabil whispered, grinning again.

"Yes, we know all about your friends and the Horde," Michal said, "and if you'll just listen to me, you'll have your opportunity to save them. They're needed as well. But you have to listen to me. It is very important that the six lost books be found by you before they land in the hands of the Dark One."

Johnis paced, confused by the sudden turn of events. "I'm not even a real fighter—this can't be right. I don't even know what these books are."

"The Books of History, lad! Everything written in them is perfect history. The first seven books crafted by Elyon, each in a different color, were bound by red twine, never to be opened except in the most terrible circumstance, because they hold a very great power. Which is why you must find them before the Dark One does."

"Do you accept?" Gabil asked, eyes bright.

"This can't be right—"

"Now you listen to me, lad." Michal walked forward, around the book, and stopped three feet from Johnis. "Why you humans fell for that beast Teeleh the first time, I'll never understand. But this is a chance for you to find yourselves again. Not only you, all of you! You're not just some random sixteen-year-old boy—you've been chosen from birth, even before the Great Deception! I expect you to accept your destiny."

For the second time this day, Johnis found himself being asked to be someone he didn't think he was. First by Thomas, now this.

He felt his face flush with frustration. What would Father say to this? He knew what Mother would say. "Run, boy. You know that anyone who goes on missions that make no sense always ends up dead."

"Will I be killed?" Johnis asked.

"Of course."

He stopped pacing, stunned. "You *know* that?"

"All humans are killed at some point," Michal said.

"And is my 'point' soon?"

Michal eyed him, then sauntered back to Gabil's side and turned around. But he didn't answer the question. "There are a few other details you will need to know. We can tell you that one of the books hides in the west."

"There aren't any forests west of here," Johnis protested. "We'd turn to Scabs without water."

"You'll *find* water," Gabil, the odder of the two, said. "Do you think we'd let such a cute face shrivel into Scab flesh?"

"Where to the west are these books?"

"We don't know," Michal said. "If we did, we wouldn't be here talking to you."

"This is impossible! We can't just head west and find six missing books in the desert! The *Horde* lives out there, for Elyon's sake."

"The Horde is the least of your worries," Michal said. "You don't believe me? Have you lost the simple belief you once had as a child?"

"I'm not saying that. I'm—"

"Yes, you are. Go west! Find your destiny. Find the books. And if you die, so be it. You've been chosen!"

A long stretch of silence separated them.

"I knew it, I knew it," Gabil whispered. "What did I tell you, Michal? He's going to accept!"

"He hasn't accepted yet," Michal mumbled.

Johnis tried to stall them. "What are the other details?"

"You'll need the other three."

"The other three hate me. I may need them, but they don't need me."

"If you can't convince them to follow you, you will pay a terrible and immediate price."

"They call me Scrapper."

"Shut your yapper, Scrapper," Gabil said, chuckling. He saw the insensitivity of his comment right away and covered his mouth with a wing. "Oh, sorry! Sorry, that wasn't nice, was it?"

So the Roush had been near enough to overhear Billos on the trail. That gave Johnis some confidence. And there was this book on the sand. And the Roush themselves, not to mention the fact that Gabil had rescued him.

"Furthermore," Michal said, "you can't breathe a word of this to anyone else, only the four of you. Do you understand? Under no circumstances will you tell any living person in this world anything you learn on your quest."

Johnis thought about it all. A faraway cry carried into the bowl.

He faced the Roush, still hot in the face. "So it's as simple as that, is it? 'Just go west and find the six missing Books of History filled with enough power to destroy all humanity, lad. Never mind that you aren't a fighter. Never mind that you're out here by mistake. Never mind that the others hate you. You've got the mark. You were chosen.'"

"Yes," Michal said.

"And how do we escape these Horde?"

Gabil leaped into the air, soared to one of the crevices that Johnis had first thought might be a way out of the bowl, landed in a somersault, and sprang to his feet. He swept his wing toward the small gap. "Here!" he cried, as if unveiling a grand prize.

Johnis walked over, gave the Roush a wide berth, and stepped up to the gap. Beyond lay the deep desert's rolling dunes. The sun was sinking directly ahead, to the west. A butterfly beat in his belly.

"And as for your friends," Gabil said, flying to the bowl's opposite end, "they're trapped in a canyon beyond this wall, through here." He pointed to a third small gap.

"This is their only escape," Michal said. "Take the book and show them this escape—surely that will be enough to convince them that you know what you're talking about."

"Then you don't know Billos or Darsal," Johnis said.

"I know humans. It's enough."

"You accept?" Gabil asked again, waddling back.

Johnis walked over to the book and picked it up, turning it in his hands. The title *Stories of History* was etched into the black leather cover, between the two straps of red twine.

"Careful, you may not want your blood to touch that book," Michal said, taking a step forward. He was staring at Johnis's finger, stained with blood from when he'd last touched his head to feel how his cut was doing. Striking Jackov head-on had left a deep wound that matted his dark hair with blood.

Without thinking Johnis touched the book with his bloodied finger. "Why not? I—"

An image slammed into his mind. A black strobe that ignited his world with darkness, even though it was still light.

The twisted image of a man or beast shrouded in a black cape. Or wings. A hat perhaps. Striding straight for him, featureless except for the capewings and an outstretched arm with long spiked fingers grasping at him, as if it wanted the book.

A loud moan, like that of a man in the throes of death, wrenched through the air. *Mmmmwwwwaaaaa . . .*

Johnis gasped and yanked his hand from the book. The image was gone. But his fingers were shaking like a rattler's tail.

"That's why," Michal said. "And don't ask what just happened because I can't tell you. It's beyond me. Beyond you. Just keep the books from blood."

Johnis was too stunned to speak.

"It's real," Michal said softly. "Will you accept this task?"

"I will," Johnis said softly. He wanted to ask about the book, but he wasn't sure what to ask.

"Good," Michal said, waddling away. "You'll see us again, don't worry. Remember, no one but you four may know of us—or the books or anything else that happens to you."

"But the Horde is going to attack," Johnis said, still feeling a bit numb. "We have to get back and report what we've seen."

For a few beats the white bat just eyed him. "Yes, the Horde. Is it better for ten thousand to die now or a hundred thousand in a month?"

Johnis blinked. "Ten thousand now, I suppose."

"Then find the books."

He asked the one question that came from his heart of hearts. "Will I live?"

"That should be none of your concern. If you die, you die for Elyon."

"But being chosen doesn't mean I'll die. Or does it?"

Gabil looked at him with sober eyes. When he spoke, his voice was soft. "Most who are chosen die, Johnis. But when the time comes, you won't care. Just try to stay alive long enough to find as many of the books as you can. Promise me that."

Johnis swallowed. "I promise."

What an absurd promise, he thought.

NINE

Our assassins are dead?" Qurong roared. "Then these four saplings had an escort?"

"No," the priest of the Horde said in his low, gravelly voice. "I don't think so."

The general stood from the table. His head brushed one of the serpent statues this cursed priest himself had hung from the tent to protect them. Four others stood in each corner of the lavish tent, gazing at him with their beady ruby eyes. Underfoot, mats dyed purple covered the smooth sand.

They were at the heart of the Horde camp, a massive field of tents hidden deep in a long desert valley to the west of the Middle Forest. The sound of clanking metal rang through the air as it

TED DEKKER

always did—swords and sickles and spears being hammered back into shape by the blacksmiths, a task made necessary because of the soft bronze they used to fashion their weapons. It was no secret that the Forest Guard used better materials in their swords, but that would soon end. The traitor was teaching them well.

In three more days they would march on the forests from the west. The spy had reported that Thomas expected them in the east. All was according to plan.

All except these four runts.

"Then how could four of our most experienced warriors fall to children?"

"They aren't children." The priest picked a fly off his arm and crushed it between his thumb and forefinger. He didn't bother wiping the innards from his skin. "But you're right, we should have had them. They were as green as seedlings."

"That's no answer. Are you telling me that they are a match for our forces?"

"No," the priest said. "They used their black magic, I would say. Trickery was involved."

"Bah! I don't care about your spells and magic. We know from the traitor that none of their attempts at magic work." Qurong clubbed his chair, breaking the spindles that had been crudely fixed as a backrest.

The priest was a sly, wicked snake. His days would end with the swing of a sword.

"I wouldn't dismiss Teeleh's power so easily," the priest said.

"Your whole point is to capture the marked one because he can lead us to the missing books."

"I want the boy only because of *their* superstitions, not mine. Thomas Hunter believes the boy will save them. Do you think he called up so many young to send them off to die? No, he was looking for the promised one, and now he thinks he's found him. Killing the boy will crush Thomas."

The high priest drilled him with a dark stare and held his gaze the way he often did. "Then you don't believe finding the seven lost Books of History will give us an advantage?"

"Did I say that?" Qurong turned from the man's crushing glare. "Show me Teeleh and I will give him my soul and find the rest of the books. But for now we fight with flesh and blood, not spells and magic."

"If I'm not mistaken, you *have* given him your soul," the priest said softly.

Qurong turned away. "It doesn't matter; we'll have these four saplings in the canyons. Send another five hundred men. If the recruits escape now, they will inform the forests that we have elite fighters on the west side. That devil Thomas will know we've fooled them with this show of force on the east."

FOUR HOURS' RIDE DUE WEST FROM WHERE QURONG'S LARGE camp hid in the desert valley, Thomas paced in one of the gazebos that overlooked the lake. Mikil, the woman he'd promoted after

Justin's recent defection, stood by the railing, watching several hundred who'd already gathered at the lake for the night's celebration.

"We should have sent spies at least," she said. "Someone to watch over them and report back."

"I have my reasons for sending them alone," Thomas shot back. "They're meant to be tested, not pampered."

"Those four are bound to tear each other apart. Or at least tear Johnis apart." She shook her head. "They're a wounded lot. I hope you know who you picked."

"I picked the four strongest candidates. You have Billos, the tempestuous bulldog who swings first and asks later; Darsal, battered and insecure inside but covers it with enough boldness to take on a whole squad on the outside; Silvie, who is the smartest recruit in the field with a burning revenge that will drive her to the end."

"Those sound like weaknesses," Mikil said.

"They are. But these fighters use their weaknesses to fuel excellence. They will be warriors because they must. The only question that remains is whether they can lead. Together."

"And the fourth? You didn't mention Johnis. Or is his weakness that he's simply not qualified?"

"He's the one who will bring the rest together or die trying."

Only he and Rachelle knew about the prophecy concerning the chosen child who would prove himself and save them all.

Today Thomas had found the child. His name was Johnis.

"You're probably right," Mikil said with a sigh. "The sun sets in two hours. They still have plenty of time."

"It's dark in three hours," Thomas said. "They have enough time to take a nap along the way."

"Unless—"

"Enough." Thomas lifted his hand. "There won't be an *unless*. How many of the Guard are pitched in the Eastern Forest?"

"All ten thousand. Leaving the rest of the forests unprotected, including the western flank, where you've sent the four new recruits."

"You're saying that we have a reason to doubt our scouts? There are enough tents out in the east to house an army of two hundred thousand Horde. That's an illusion?"

"Not my point, sir." Mikil said. "I'm just worried about the four you sent off alone. We hardly have enough Guard to mount a rescue if they did run into trouble."

Thomas nodded but held his jaw firm. He knew that sending them off so close to a major battle wasn't entirely sane. But he also knew that one of those four had been chosen. Perhaps he had to know. Perhaps he'd intentionally sent Johnis off with three scrappers, knowing that he would be tested.

"As I said, I have my reasons," he said. "What worries me more is the battle we will throw them into when they return." He sighed. "I want you to take the thousand new recruits to the eastern flank at first light with all the resin from our reserves. They can help finish the trenches and pour the resin. When the battle comes, they will man the torches and spring the traps. I don't want them in battle this time. It's too early."

He'd come up with the notion of digging deep trenches in the sand and filling them with flammable resin from the nanka tree. The Horde would ride their horses into a firestorm, if it worked as well as he hoped.

Mikil's eyes twinkled. "That's"—she hesitated—"a good idea, sir. The recruits are too raw to fight."

"No, you're wrong," he said, walking out of the gazebo. "They're not too young. But I can't bear the thought of any dying so soon."

TEN

Johnis was forced to lift his legs up by the saddle so his horse could make it through the narrow gap the two Roush had directed him to before flying off in a rush. He expected the sounds of fighting but could hear only the hollow whistle of wind through the canyons.

The blue sky above was turning red, as it did every evening over the desert. Johnis's palms were slimy with sweat, and he couldn't shake the chills that spread down from his neck.

He still couldn't truly believe all that he'd heard. Or the flash he'd felt when he touched the book. Alone here in the rocks, with the sky turning red and the Horde scouring the canyons, the idea of heading out into the desert in search of six lost books seemed like suicide.

And the notion that he was chosen by Elyon to undertake this quest was the most ridiculous thing he'd ever heard.

He wasn't brave.

He wasn't strong.

He wasn't crafty.

He wasn't even very smart.

Even if he was one of those things, he wasn't ready to die, which was the only thing Michal had said that made sense.

If he went into the desert, he would die sooner or later, probably sooner. If the Horde didn't get him first, he would die from the disease. Without the lake to bathe in, his skin would crack open, his eyes would turn gray, and he would writhe in pain on the hot desert sand.

Johnis stopped the horse at the end of the crevice, held his breath, and listened for any sign of Horde or the others. Something knocked a few pebbles off a ledge to his right. His pulse spiked, then eased when he saw a blue lizard scamper into a crack. Nothing else.

He let his breath out slowly.

He wasn't sure where he was in these canyons, but he could probably find a way back to the forest to tell Thomas everything. That's what he would do.

Of course that's what he'd do. He had no choice. Anything else would be irresponsible. He couldn't go looking for the others only to get himself killed. He had to warn Thomas. There were elite Scab fighters on the west who knew more than they should.

There was a spy in the forest. Someone who bathed in the lakes but was really a Scab at heart. That was the meaning of what he'd seen when he had touched book. An evil omen, if it had happened at all.

Johnis leaned over the black stallion and rubbed its neck. "Shh, shh, shh. Stay quiet, boy." He nudged its flanks and walked out into the canyon, guiding the animal over the areas of thickest sand.

The canyon came to a T, but the left channel was blocked by fallen boulders. Johnis guided the stallion to his right around a large boulder, sweating now, begging Elyon that no Scabs would be waiting so he could make his way out, back to the forests, back home.

There was no Horde.

Instead, there were three Forest Guard fighters: Billos, Darsal, and Silvie. They had dismounted and were holed up behind a rock, keeping their horses muzzled.

Johnis pulled up. This was the worst of all possible developments, he realized. If Billos and the others were hunkered down in hiding, then there was no escape. There were obviously Scabs in the canyon beyond the boulders.

The moment Billos saw Johnis coming up from behind, his eyes widened, and he frantically motioned for him to get along the cliff wall.

Johnis instinctively ducked and moved his horse to the cliff. He slipped off and led the beast forward. Silvie's bright eyes followed him in. Darsal looked stern but not frightened. Billos, on the other hand, looked furious. And no wonder—in his mind, Johnis had run off to save his own skin again.

Johnis was tempted to leave them and hurry back the way he'd come, through the crevice into the bowl and out into the desert by himself. He would find another way back to the forest.

But then something happened that changed Johnis's heart in the space of one breath. Silvie, the short, beautiful fighter with blond hair and bright blue eyes, winked at him.

She'd winked at him. Why, he had no clue. They were in a canyon, trapped by Horde, and she'd drilled him with her blue eyes and winked.

He was so startled by her wink that he stopped five feet from them. Her flawless face glistened with sweat, and her cheekbones were smudged. She lifted a single finger to her lips, signaling silence.

Johnis acted spontaneously then, letting his instincts take over, thinking, he told himself, with his heart. He waved Silvie forward with his hand. Then more urgently when she hesitated.

She left her horse and stepped up to him, keeping her blue eyes on his. He motioned her closer, and she came near enough for him to smell the gardenia blossoms that many of the women in the village used to scent their necks.

He leaned forward so that his mouth brushed the hair over her right ear. "Tell the others to follow me," he whispered. "If they want to live, follow me."

Then, without looking to see what her response was, he turned and led his horse back the way he'd come.

No matter how tempted he was to look back, he refused. Either they would follow, or he would go alone. Into the bowl, into the desert, then back around to the forest and home. Maybe even run into a few catalina cacti along the way.

He turned the corner, walked another fifty feet, and pulled up. Now he looked back. No sign of Billos and company scurrying after him.

Another ten seconds and still no sign. They probably hadn't budged. He thought about going back for at least Silvie. If he explained . . .

She suddenly came around the bend, leading her horse. And behind her Billos, then Darsal.

"This is a dead end; we've been here!" Billos whispered as they came close. "We'll be rats in a crate if the Scabs come this way. Our position at the rock at least gave us a fighting chance."

"Then go back," Johnis said. He looked at Silvie. "I've found a hidden passage out of this canyon. You can join me if you want, but we have to hurry."

Without waiting for any response, he turned away and continued down the canyon.

"The scrapper's lying," Billos whispered.

"Then go back," Silvie returned.

Darsal searched Billos's eyes. "Maybe he's onto something, Billos."

Johnis felt his heart lighten. Darsal had sided with him? She was no fool; he'd known that from the beginning. None of them were, but facing death had a way of slowing your thinking. Maybe that was the difference between him and Billos. When faced with death, Johnis's mind worked better, faster. Billos's, like most, slowed.

Then again, maybe not.

He led them into the crevice, feeling as strong as he had all day. *There is now true hope,* he thought. They were going to get home tonight, alive and well.

Billos and the others sat on their horses and scanned the large, empty bowl. No Shataiki, no Roush, just a hiding spot in the middle of the canyons. Now that Johnis thought about it, he hadn't seen the black Shataiki bats on the cliffs since the Roush had left.

"How did you find this place?" Darsal asked.

"A gap in the rocks over there." Johnis pointed back to the entrance through which he'd first come. "But I think there are Scabs on the other side."

"Then they'll find the same hole you did," Billos said. "This could be a trap."

"Better than being trapped behind a rock," Silvie said. "If they come after us, we can kill them one by one as they squeeze through the opening."

"The Horde won't find the hole easily," Johnis said. "But we can't stay here. Follow me."

"Just hold up, Scrapper," Billos snapped. "How do you know the Horde won't find the hole if you did?"

Johnis threw caution to the wind and told them then. "I didn't find it. A Roush named Gabil led me to it."

They looked at him as if he'd just suggested that the Horde were figments of their imagination and that the Forest Guard had been mistakenly fighting sand all these years. Even Silvie showed no belief. But she did give him some benefit of doubt. "Really? How so?"

He told them the whole story, everything except the fact that he was marked with a circle with two slash marks and chosen for this mission—because he didn't believe that himself. That and the bit about the book's reaction to blood.

When he finished, they just looked at him with eyes that made it clear they were convinced they were looking at a lunatic.

"I know, it sounds crazy. But I think there might be something to it." As he said it, he realized he was arguing for something that just minutes ago had sounded as absurd to him.

"You're trying to tell us that a fuzzy white bat told you to take us all on a quest to find the six lost Books of History?" Billos demanded. "Do you realize how absolutely mad that sounds?"

He looked at Silvie, but she wasn't defending him now.

"Yes, I realize that. And do you realize that I've just rescued you?"

"Have you, now?"

"We're standing in a bowl carved from the canyons, for the sake of Elyon!" Johnis said. "How else could I have found it?"

"You stumbled on it, obviously. The Horde is gathering on the east, you fool! You think we should desert the Guard on account of this nonsense? It would be treasonous!"

Johnis tossed open his saddlebag and pulled out the bound Book of History, careful not to touch it with his bloodstained finger. He shoved it at them. "And what about this?"

Their eyes settled on the black leather book.

"Tell me where I found this," Johnis demanded.

Silvie stepped up and took the book gingerly. Her finger traced the title etched in leather. "*Stories of History,*" she said softly. "I think this is real."

"It could be one of his books," Billos said. "A book of poetry. Open it."

Johnis took the book back. "You can't. The book has too much power. They warned me against opening it. They also claimed that if I wasn't able to convince you to follow me, something terrible would happen. Immediately." He wrapped the book in a cloth and set it back in his saddlebag.

"This is all fine and well," Darsal said, "but are you ready to take off into the desert, directly west, without water for your skin, to take on the Horde because two fuzzy white bats told you to?"

"Do we have a choice?"

"There *are* no fuzzy white bats!" Billos cried.

A distant horn moaned through the desert. They glanced west.

"There you have it," Darsal said. "Going west is suicide."

"Johnis is right about one thing," Silvie said. "The Horde knows we're here, and they're not taking it lightly."

"The only way they could know . . ." Darsal's voice trailed off.

"Is through a spy in the forest," Silvie finished.

Not even Billos argued this point.

"Say what you want, Billos," Silvie continued, "coward or not, Johnis hasn't been wrong yet."

The seventeen-year-old scowled. "So you're ready to abandon Thomas and run after these supposedly lost books?"

"No, but you need to use your head a little more."

With that, they plunged into a round of argument that Johnis was content to watch in silence. Silvie defended him but still didn't seem to actually believe his story. Darsal defended Billos but didn't seem too comfortable with his suggestion that they turn back immediately and finish their mission.

After a good ten minutes of bickering, Darsal settled the matter.

"Listen to me, you young Guard pups!" She was saying it to all of them, but she was looking at Johnis. "We can't abandon our supreme commander for a story of two fuzzy white bats that we all know don't exist. We have to get back and report this clear danger. For all we know, the Horde is preparing to attack from this side of the forest. And if they do that, with all of our forces on the east, the Middle Forest will be annihilated! As the oldest, I'm taking charge. We go back!"

Without waiting for consensus, Billos leaped into his saddle and started toward the gap in the far wall where Johnis had first come in. "Follow me."

In his confusion, Johnis was the last to mount. "Remember what Michal warned," he said, taking up the rear.

"Yes, we know," Billos said, "a terrible thing immediately. What this bat forgot to tell you is that the terrible thing happened three hours ago when Thomas chose you to be one of the Guard."

They followed Billos through the narrow passage and out into the canyon where Johnis had been trapped. No Horde.

"This is the canyon you came down, Johnis?" Darsal whispered.

"Yes."

"We go to the left ahead," Billos said.

Eeeaaaaouuu . . .

Johnis jerked his head up at the screech. The cliffs were lined with Shataiki again. Watching them with red eyes like vultures waiting for the kill.

"I don't think this is a good idea," Johnis whispered, trying not to sound frantic.

"Maybe he's right," Silvie said.

"We can't abandon Thomas!" Darsal snapped.

So they walked on. Toward the mouth of the canyon.

They all heard the distant thundering of hooves at the same time, but Darsal was the first to throw up a hand. "Stop!"

Johnis stood in his saddle and looked around the corner into the main canyon. The black Horde stormed toward them from two hundred yards out. Not just a dozen or two, but hundreds.

"Back! Back!" Darsal cried.

"Follow me!" Johnis cried, whipping his horse around. They had to get back into the bowl. Silvie was already riding hard beside him, and just to her rear, Darsal.

But Billos had hesitated.

They took the corner into the smaller canyon at a full sprint, horse hooves sliding on the sandy floor. But the sure-footed animals would not fall.

Billos was last, and the Horde were close, far too close for comfort.

"Hurry!" Johnis screamed. He slapped the stallion's rump with the flat of his hand until his palm stung. The huge black beast pounded toward the dead end ahead.

Johnis pulled up sharply and jerked the reins to the right, forcing the animal around the boulder and into the crevice that appeared out of nowhere.

The clacking of his horse's hooves echoed off the narrow walls. "Did they make it?" he asked, twisting back.

"Did Billos make it?" Silvie asked Darsal.

"Not yet, he's still—"

Billos's roar carried into the passage, cutting her short. Then a grunt. Then nothing.

All three of them stopped in the narrow passage, panting. Horde yells carried past them. Then one last muted yell from Billos.

Johnis urged his horse forward, into the bowl. He pulled to one side and waited for Silvie and Darsal to squeeze through. The moment Darsal had cleared the passage, she spun her horse around and headed back in.

"No!" Silvie snapped. "There are too many!"

Darsal pulled up short, her horse stamping. Silvie was right, of course. There had to be a hundred of the Horde stuffed into the small canyon, searching for the three Forest Guard who'd vanished by magic.

But it wasn't magic, and the Scabs would eventually find the opening.

Movement at the bowl's rim caught Johnis's eye. Michal sat there watching them, looking stately. And beside him, Gabil, bouncing a little.

Silvie followed Johnis's eyes, saw nothing, and faced him.

"Are you with me?" Johnis asked.

Darsal spit to one side, pulling her horse in a tight circle. Her eyes were on the passage that led to Billos, or what was left of him.

"He's alive," she said. "He's not easily killed. We can't leave him!"

"If he's alive, the Horde will take him to their camp," Johnis said. "That camp is out in the desert. West."

Darsal eyed him angrily, as if Billos's fate was in his hands. "I will not abandon him!"

"What do you suggest?" he asked.

"We go after him! We rescue him! For the love of Elyon, we don't abandon him!"

"Then we may all die. These are impossible odds. You went against me once, and look what it cost. You're wanting to try again?"

"You cocky little runt!"

"I . . . Forgive me, I don't know what else to tell you."

Silvie was looking west. "You're sure about this, Johnis?"

"You said the book looked real, didn't you? I found this bowl, didn't I? We've paid terribly for your not listening the first time, haven't we? If I wasn't sure before, I am now."

Darsal grunted. Clearly every last fiber of her being wanted to race back after Billos.

"They'll find the opening," Johnis said. "Then we'll all be dead."

"Billos is not dead!" Darsal yelled. Her voice echoed.

"And now the Horde knows that we're nearby," Johnis said. He slapped his horse and shot toward the passageway leading to the red desert. "But you're right, Darsal—Billos isn't dead."

"Is that so?" she said angrily, still unmoving behind Silvie, who had started her horse after Johnis.

"Yes, that is so. I know it is so because the fuzzy white bats that don't exist told me that all four of us were needed."

Silence.

Johnis peered into the passage and saw the desert sand waiting. A dozen black Shataiki winged their way through the red sky.

He turned back. "We need Billos, and now Billos needs us."

With that Johnis headed into the passage.

ELEVEN

I t's dark," Rachelle said, speaking the obvious to her husband. "You can't keep this up forever."

"That will be my judgment, not yours."

She smiled gently in the darkness, unbothered by his stubbornness. Annoying at times, but one of the qualities that made him the great leader he'd become over the last ten years.

Three of his officers—Mikil, William, and Suzan—stood with crossed arms on his right, as he paced impatiently in the war room, housed in the barracks to the south of the great amphitheater. From here they could see hundreds of flaming torches around the lake. A ring of gazebos circled the upper shores of the large body of water, seven of which were reserved for council, all now empty.

Dancers twirled around the fires, moving to music from wood flutes and drums. They all knew the beating drums carried far into the forest to the ears of any Scab scouts sneaking through the darkness, but this only encouraged them. The Horde should know that the Forest Dwellers danced in the face of their threat.

Though thousands gathered for this show of celebration, as they did every evening, a sense of defeat hung over the village, Rachelle thought. Death was coming in three days. Four at the most. If the Horde broke past the eastern defenses and the wall of fire that Thomas intended to ignite, they would sweep into the village, forcing every man, woman, and child to take up a sword.

Something had to change. They couldn't keep the Horde back forever. In the last major battle, more than two thousand had fallen, forcing Thomas to call up the younger ones as he had. But surely they couldn't pin their hopes on a thousand sixteen- and seventeen-year-olds.

"They've been held up," Thomas said. "Probably dropped a cactus and had to go back for more."

"The army is expecting you on the eastern front," Mikil said, standing. "I told you we should have sent an escort!"

Marie, Thomas's twelve-year-old daughter, ran up to the outlook and took the steps two at a time. Her cotton tunic flapped around thin tanned legs. Her hair was drawn back in a ponytail, and she wore a leather fighting helmet, too large for her head. She and her friends had been recounting the football game played by the recruits earlier, no doubt.

"Are they back, Father?" she cried.

"Not yet, dear," Rachelle answered.

From the darkness flew another child, and Thomas's heart fell when he saw who she was. Johnis's younger sister, Kiella, a friend to Marie.

"Tell her it's not true," Kiella said, running up.

"What's not true?" Rachelle asked.

Marie answered in a loud voice. "Samuel says they are dead. Tell me it's not true."

At ten years old, Thomas's son, Samuel, was full of vinegar like his father, Rachelle thought. "Don't be ridiculous," she said, brushing dirt from her daughter's chin.

"That's what I told him. No Forest Guard would let the Scabs kill them on their first day! But he says Johnis isn't really a Forest Guard and likely got them in trouble. Now they're being eaten for stew."

"He said that?" Thomas asked. "Tell him that I say who the Forest Guard is, not him. Tell him Johnis will one day save his skinny neck!"

"Easy, dear," Rachelle whispered.

"And then tell him I love him more than I love my own life. I would never put him in danger by choosing the wrong fighter to protect our home."

"It's dark," a man said, walking in. It was Ramos, Johnis's father. And he looked worried.

Rachelle exchanged a glance with Thomas and saved the

children from hearing what might be exchanged by taking Kiella's chin in her fingers. "Your brother is a hero, Kiella. And he'll return to a hero's welcome."

Kiella's eyes widened. She brushed past her father, flew down the steps, and ran into the darkness, Marie hard on her heels.

"Where are they?" Ramos asked. "It's dark."

Thomas bit the inside of his cheek, then said what he always said when faced with the families of his fighters: the truth. "We don't know where they are."

Ramos's eyes bugged. "Don't know. You mean they're lost?"

"We don't know."

Ramos's face reddened as the implications settled in. "Lost" meant hurt or wounded or dead. There was no such thing as lost in the forest. They all knew it like the knots in a Horde ball.

He shoved his large hand toward the west. "Then find him!"

"Easy, Ramos," Rachelle said. "We will find him."

"Now! Find my son! You sent him out, you bring him back. For Elyon's sake, don't just stand here!"

"Please remember who you're talking to," Mikil snapped.

Ramos caught himself, took a deep breath, and settled down. "Forgive me. I lost myself. But they will be okay, you think."

"I think they're probably struggling with four large catalina cacti right now, arguing over whose fault it is that they dropped one," Thomas said.

A crooked grin split the man's face. "That would be them. Not Johnis, but the others. Thank you, sir." He dipped his head. "And forgive my indiscretion." He took Thomas's hand, bowed to it, then hurried off into the night. "It's okay," Thomas could hear Ramos say to someone. "They're on the way back."

He turned away and faced the dark lake.

"What do we do?" Mikil asked.

"We go after them."

Mikil stepped up and lowered her arms. "The Horde is gathered and ready to march on the east. We can't compromise our defenses on account of four recruits."

"We go after them!" Thomas whispered harshly. "These are not just any four recruits."

Surely Mikil knows there is no sense arguing with Thomas when it comes to matters of loyalty, Rachelle thought. *Then again, she is fairly new in her promotion.*

"I remember rescuing you once, when you were left with a spear in your side," Thomas said to Mikil in a low voice.

That stopped her short. She dipped her head. "Forgive me. I'm indebted to you always."

"Gather one hundred of our best fighters," Thomas said. "We leave within the hour."

TWELVE

S top!" Darsal cried. Her voice rang out over the desert dunes. "For Elyon's mad love, stop this!"

Johnis eased the reins back and faced her. A round, red moon that gave little light hung large over her head. Silvie pulled up just in front of her.

Darsal lowered her voice. "For the last time, I really do think we should reconsider this," she said, glancing around at the empty dunes.

The desert air was quiet. No Horde, no Shataiki, no lizards, nothing but them and their horses. But they all knew nothing could be farther from the truth. The forests had disappeared from sight an hour ago, and Johnis's courage had begun to fade as well.

"You can't possibly think that this makes any sense," Darsal said. She seemed to have changed without Billos by her side. Her eyes moved nervously, and she repeatedly scanned the dark desert, not for Horde but for Billos, if Johnis guessed correctly. It made him wonder what had created this bond they shared.

"You chose to follow me," he said. "And if you like, you can choose to turn back now."

"I came because the Horde were climbing up our backside and Billos was taken," Darsal snapped. "What did you expect from me under such pressure?"

"To go after Billos with me," Johnis said.

"We're not going after Billos! We're headed to the end of the world. No one's ever crossed this desert and returned alive."

"Michal was quite clear," Johnis insisted. "He said directly west, so we go directly west."

She pulled her horse up next to his. "Then look directly west. What do you see?"

He scanned the black horizon. In all honesty, he hardly felt more confident than she did. It was so dark he couldn't tell where the sand stopped and the sky began.

"If it's any comfort, I'm not enjoying this either," he said quietly. He took a deep breath and let it out slowly, thinking that maybe now was a good time to tell them the rest of what the Roush had said.

But Darsal spoke first. "I don't care whether or not you're enjoying this. The question is whether or not you've lost the few peanuts contained in that container above your shoulders. I think we should turn back and report Billos's fate now before it's too late."

Johnis clenched his jaw and headed down the dune. "And abandon Billos?"

She muttered a curse and plunged down after him.

He had to stop this bickering of hers. The path they were on was frightening enough without her throwing doubt at them at every step. The image that had crashed through him when he touched the book filled his mind. Maybe he should cut Darsal's finger and force her to touch the book and then see what he had seen. Silvie too. They would surely agree then.

But the Roush had said it was dangerous to touch blood to the books. Had warned him not to, which just as surely meant not to make it common knowledge. That's why he'd decided not to share this experience.

But he had to try something to get Darsal off his back. If not for the fact that Michal had insisted he would need all of them, he would send her away rather than try to convince her to stay with him.

Reason was the only way. Reason *with* heart. Perhaps he could force her to think with her heart if he matched her insistence with his own. He should be stronger, not more understanding. In honesty, he was already being nearly as strong as he dared, but it clearly wasn't enough.

"You will follow me, Darsal," Johnis said as she pulled up.

Then he said something that sounded offensive even to him—he had to; he saw no other choice. "You will follow me to hell itself if that's where I lead you."

Even Silvie seemed taken aback by his boldness. "She may have a point, Johnis. You know we could still cut back and make it to the forests in the darkness."

"But we won't," he said, holding firm. "We can't. Our destiny is out here in the desert of death where the Horde lie in wait, desperate to feed on our flesh."

"Of all the . . ." Darsal was fuming. "You're speaking like an idiot, Scrapper! We came this far because . . ." She paused, searching for words to make her case. "Okay, you *did* say a few things that made sense, I'll admit that. And Billos *was* taken. But that doesn't mean you have to lord it over us, for the love of . . ." She spit to one side.

"You'll follow me to the moon and back, Darsal," Johnis said in a soft voice. "You might as well get used to it."

He knew he sounded like a jerk, but he had his reasons.

They rode in silence for a few minutes, perhaps only because Darsal was so taken aback by his sudden change in tone. The sandy dunes gave way to hard, flat ground that had been baked by the sun.

Then Darsal started up again. "Okay, I really think—"

"If I tell you to march off the end of the earth, you will, Darsal," Johnis interrupted.

"Of all the—"

"If I tell you to dig a hole and bury yourself in the hot sand, you will, and you'll do it singing my praise," Johnis said.

Darsal stopped. "I will not!" she screamed.

Johnis spun back. "Of course you won't!" he said. "But the question you have to ask yourself is, what *will* you do?"

Silvie reached out a hand. "Johnis . . ."

"You too, Silvie. What will you do? Ask yourselves now, once and for all, what you will do, because I can't live with this bickering for days on end."

They looked at him, dumbstruck, not understanding.

He sighed. "I was rescued by two Roush who told me that I was chosen, along with you, to find the six lost Books of History. And believe me, I didn't like what they told me one bit. What they asked me to do was the same as jumping off the end of the earth, as far as I was concerned. Like burying my head in the sand, ignoring reason. But I had to make a choice."

Now did they get it? Darsal blinked. Silvie held his gaze.

"They said you should follow me off this cliff, and I'm staking my life on the hope that you will," he continued. "But you have to decide. Will you follow me, Darsal? Will you, Silvie? Will you both follow me to hell and back because two fuzzy white bats told me you should?"

The desert rang with his demand. He'd shocked them into a new frame of mind, he thought. A brilliant piece of manipulation. This was why he was their leader now instead of Billos—or Darsal or Silvie, for that matter.

"Go bury your head in the sand and light your backside on fire for all I care," Darsal said.

But she didn't turn and ride for the forests. She rode her horse forward, deeper into the night, deeper into the desert.

Johnis could see the smirk on Silvie's face despite the darkness. She, at least, found some pleasure in his quick thinking.

They rode in silence for another two hours, and Johnis was content to let Darsal lead them. It gave her a sense of purpose apart from finding Billos, something she desperately needed. Silvie came next, and once more he took up the rear.

When Darsal held up her hand to stop them, announcing that they had to get some sleep, he simply plopped off his horse, unrolled his blanket, and lay down before either of them had a chance to dismount.

"Tie your horse's reins to your ankle so it won't abandon us," Silvie told him, throwing her blanket near him. "Do you want to walk home?"

"We're not going home," he said.

Darsal humphed. "If we don't find water at first light, we are."

Johnis did as Silvie instructed and lay back down, using his arms as a pillow. "We will find water."

"How do you know?"

"Because Michal said we would."

"The fuzzy white bat speaks again," Darsal quipped.

"And was there anything else the Roush told you that you haven't bothered to mention?" Silvie asked, lying three feet from him. To preserve body heat, the Forest Guard normally slept side by side if caught out in the desert, but she didn't seem eager to follow the practice.

"They told me two things," Johnis said.

Darsal grunted and slumped to the ground on his other side. "Wonderful."

He was now flanked by two beautiful, grumpy women. Wonderful indeed.

"Well?" Silvie pressed. "What did they tell you?"

Johnis cleared his throat. "The first thing they told me was that I was chosen at birth to save all of you."

Silence.

"The second was that I will die."

THIRTEEN

There had been that time when his younger brother had broken six ostrich eggs into a bowl and forgotten about them in the woodshed. A week later the smell had raised cries of outrage from three houses down, so foul was the stench. It was the same year that Billos had first met Darsal.

The year when both of their lives had changed one very ugly afternoon.

This was the odor that filled Billos's nostrils now. The smell of sulfur and rotten eggs and maggots, all rolled into one terrible perfume.

Horde breath.

His left arm was hurt, maybe broken. A lucky sword thrust by their captain had knocked him from his horse as he'd been riding after Darsal in the canyon.

His first thought upon landing in the sand was one of gratefulness at being alive—the sword could have taken his head off.

His second thought was one of doom—they were on him, and his horse was bucking ten feet away. Worse, his sword was on that bucking horse.

Still, he'd put up a courageous fight, charging the onrushing Horde on foot, dodging the first Scab before taking a club to the side of his head from out of nowhere.

His world had gone black then. Even when he awoke much later, he wasn't sure if he really was awake. There was no light, and it took him a good minute or two to realize that there was a bag over his head.

Slowly his senses came to him. And so did the smell.

He was in a Horde camp. By the sounds of the widespread laughter and the distant baying of dogs, it was a sizable camp, maybe even a city.

He was on his back, and his hands and legs were bound around a pole, like a pig being carried to the slaughter.

With his senses now intact, the meaning of his position began to settle on him. Billos was a captive of the Horde, alive for now but soon to be dead. The Horde never let captives live. They took what information they could from them through torture, then cut off their heads with a broadsword.

Thomas Hunter's stern warning to the thousand gathered

recruits still rang in his ears. "Never be taken alive," he'd roared. "Never! They'll skin you alive and you'll wish you'd never been born. Fight to the death."

Fighting a sudden bout of panic, Billos tested the ropes that bound his wrists around the pole.

He was rewarded with a boot to his ribs, and he grunted in pain.

"The worm is trying to wriggle free," a gruff voice laughed. "I say we bleed it now."

"Qurong wants it alive," said another with more authority.

"They say you can bleed it alive and it won't die," the first voice said, kicking Billos again. "It isn't human."

Something touched his hand. "Not even human," the Scab breathed.

The warrior was rubbing Billos's fist with his scaly, diseased paw. It had never occurred to him that Scab palms were cracked and rough like the rest of their skin. Nausea washed over him.

"Leave it be," a third Scab ordered. "Qurong wants to question it."

Qurong! He'd heard the name of the Horde general many times. Elyon help him, he was being taken to the monster himself!

Billos felt true fear for the first time that day. Seeing so much fighting as a boy destined for the Guard he'd found it was easy to become hardened to the threat of death. They were all destined to die anyway, it was said. It was only a question of how many Horde you managed to kill before you died.

But lying here on his back, with a bag over his head and Horde breath choking him, Billos realized that he didn't want to die. He was far too young to die! Only seventeen.

He hadn't even married yet. He hadn't owned his own house. He hadn't fought in his first battle, not really, unless you counted the encounter with the four Scabs in the forest earlier.

Billos regretted not accepting the proposal of marriage from Sebrina, an eighteen-year-old looker who'd taken a mighty fancy to him last summer when he was only sixteen. His father had discouraged him, saying that it wasn't wise for a boy destined for the Forest Guard to marry too young, before he became skillful enough in battle to survive a few years. The forests had far too many widows left by overeager young fighters, he'd said.

Now Billos cursed the Forest Guard and all that had put him in this predicament in which he was about to die unmarried!

"Then let's take it to Qurong and be done with it," the second voice said. "Its smell is making me sick."

The flap of a canvas curtain silenced them. Boots shuffled forward. *We must be in a tent,* Billos thought.

"Take a look, sir," a new voice said.

Someone scoffed, as if offended by the presence of this new *sir.* The scoff was immediately followed by a hard slap.

"Show respect," the new voice said.

Someone pulled the bag up to expose Billos's head. They *were* in a tent. Dirt floor, flaming torches. Several Scabs staring at him, close enough for him to smell every breath.

A man dressed in a black robe stepped up to him. Orange

torchlight lit the face of a Scab who stared down at Billos. The robed man wore a hood over his head, his diseased face hidden in shadows. But even so, Billos was struck by a sense of familiarity.

He'd seen this man.

But that was impossible. He'd never seen a live Scab before today, and this wasn't one of the Scab warriors from the canyons.

"Teeleh's breath, I cannot stand the sight of that traitor," one of the original Scabs hissed.

Billos had seen enough Scab meat today to fill a dozen nightmares, but here in the confines of a closed tent, their appearance made him ill. Flaking skin, yellowed by the torches. This one had a large nose, plastered with the powdery "morst" they used to ease the pain of their cracked skin, but blood or some other fluid seeped through the white powder. His muscles bulged, hardened by countless battles, no doubt, slaying the Guard. The man's imposing form sent a chill through Billos's bones.

Another Scab stepped up, jerked the sack back over his head, and spit. "If you hope to live out the year, you'd better hold your tongue. He's one of us now."

A defector from the Forest Guard, Billos thought. *No wonder the Horde has made so many advances lately. A traitorous Forest Guard fighter is feeding them information!*

"We take it to Qurong at first light," someone said.

And then it sounded as though they left the tent, leaving Billos alone, hog-tied to a pole with a bag over his head.

He lay shivering in the night air, further chilled by the cooling of his sweat. A hundred thoughts worked their way through Billos's mind, and not a single one brought him any comfort.

For a while he tried to conjure up what the others might try for a rescue, but he soon dismissed any hope in his comrades. They would be fools to head into the desert to find him, and the only true fool among them was the runt, Johnis, who was also a coward.

He tried to imagine that this business about Johnis meeting the Roush was true, but he couldn't manage it. Even children knew that Roush were myths created by the council elder, Ciphus, to promote the Great Romance, this religion that had the Forest Dwellers eating out of the palm of his hand.

Billos lay exhausted and trembling late into the night and finally, after many hours, slipped into sleep.

He'd been in the land of nightmares for just a short time when a soft ripping sound woke him. He caught his breath and jerked his head to the right.

A soft giggle sounded far off, then the howl of desert wolves. Nothing else. He was just starting to relax when the sound came again, very slowly, as if a knife was stuck in the canvas and was snapping threads one by one.

Riiiiiiiiiippppp . . .

Billos froze like a skewered pig. Darsal! She'd come for him!

Riiiiiiiippppppp . . .

The sound hissed in the night. But, no, that hissing wasn't coming from inside the tent, he realized. The hiss came from beyond the tent wall, made by whoever was cutting the canvas.

Or *whate*ver was cutting it.

"Hello?" Billos managed in a whisper.

The sound stopped. But the cutting resumed within seconds. There could be no doubt about it—someone was cutting through the canvas.

Billos heard them cut the tent. Heard them slide inside. Heard their deep, deep breathing as not one but several *someones* walked about him, feet slowly padding on the ground.

He held his breath until stars began to pop in his eyes, and then he sucked in air as quietly as he could. The moment he did, the putrid stench of Horde drove up his nostrils and lodged itself in his sinuses. He gasped and tried to breathe the smell out, but he also needed wind, so he was forced to suck it deep into his lungs.

Evidently unbothered by his sucking and fussing, whoever had come slowly lifted the pole he was bound to off the ground. He hung from his wrists and ankles, like a sack of taro root.

And then they were moving. Through the tent wall.

Through the Horde camp.

Into the desert.

Into the night.

FOURTEEN

DAY TWO

Johnis woke to a buzzing fly near his ear and the blazing sun in his eye. Without moving from his back, he gazed slowly about the camp.

His stallion stood black against the pale desert, still tied to his ankle. *The horse will need water, and soon,* he thought. But Billos's horse had been carrying the extra water jug. They each had a large canteen of lake water to either drink or bathe with, but that wouldn't last the day.

It was said that the skin disease came on so quickly in part because of the dry desert heat.

Silvie stood by her brown stallion, cinching up her saddle. The sun shone through her short blond hair, giving her a glow that reminded Johnis of a gardenia blossom. As he looked at Silvie now, working with strong arms, her smooth jaw flexing—she was stunning.

"You'll want a kind woman with spirit," his father had often advised him. "Beauty is in a woman's words as much as in her skin." Johnis moved his eyes to Darsal's horse. But Darsal's horse wasn't where it had been last night. He sat up and looked about.

"Where's Darsal?" he demanded, seeing no sign of her.

Silvie gave her saddle cinch one last tug. "I don't know. She was gone when I woke."

"Gone?" Johnis jumped to his feet. "What do you mean, gone?"

"I mean, as in not here. Her tracks lead that way." She nodded at the rising sun. East. Home.

"She just left us?"

"Evidently. What did you expect, kisses in the morning?"

"No, but she can't just up and leave."

"But she can and did," Silvie said, drilling him with her bright blue eyes. "And don't think I'm not considering the same."

Johnis felt his heart fall into the pit of his stomach. "Then everything will be lost. You can't!"

"Why, because we have to save the world? Find these lost books of yours?"

"Forget saving the world," Johnis snapped. "I don't care about saving the world either, believe me. And they're not *my* books. But by leaving us, Darsal has put herself in terrible trouble. You heard what the Roush said about Billos. And he was taken. You don't think the Horde are waiting back there for Darsal?"

"I heard what *you* said the Roush said about us," Silvie said. "And it's the only reason I haven't left you myself. But I don't see how going further into the desert is any better than facing the Horde in the canyons. I'd rather die fighting Horde than baking to a crisp in the sun."

"We'll *find* water!" Johnis yelled.

Silvie blinked at his outburst.

Darsal's voice rang out behind them. "We'd better, Scrapper!" She drove her horse down the dune from the south. "Because there's a line of Horde marching toward us from the east."

Silvie flung herself into her saddle, rode up the rise facing east, and studied the horizon. "You're sure?"

"Would I be here if I wasn't sure? I don't think they saw me, but we'd better be gone when they get here." She frowned at Johnis. "You satisfied?"

"About the Roush being right about the terrible trouble we would be in if you didn't all follow me, or about the Horde coming our way?"

She held his stare long enough for Johnis to wish he hadn't been so clever, then kneed her horse on, heading west.

They traveled deeper into the desert, three abreast for two hours, before drinking and giving the horses some water from their canteens. Twice Darsal had doubled back to see if the Horde was still following. Twice she'd returned saying they were. They should cut north or south, she insisted.

"No, the desert ahead is safer," Johnis argued. "If there were

Horde ahead of us, the ones behind wouldn't bring such a large force to drive us forward into a trap—certainly not for just three scrappers. Clearly the desert ahead is free of the beasts."

"Free of beasts and any other living thing," Darsal returned. "Including us soon. It's not surprising that no one's crossed this blasted dust bowl and survived."

"You had your chance to turn back," Silvie snapped. "Don't make it worse on us by griping all the way."

Darsal grunted and plowed reluctantly on. But Silvie seemed to be coming his way, Johnis thought. Or at the very least she wasn't set against him.

"I'm sorry for yelling at you this morning," Johnis told her, encouraged by her support. "I had no business being so rude."

"Don't think I like this," she said. "I'll head back and kill some of those Scabs before I die."

She seemed adamant about avenging her mother's death. He felt pity for her but understood the sentiment. "You must have loved your mother and father very much," he said.

Silvie frowned and turned her head away from him. "Both were lieutenants in the Guard when I was twelve, but they couldn't bear to be without me, so they both stepped into the reserves and took time guiding me through my special studies. My mother wasn't supposed to be on duty the day she was killed. It was my fault."

"Yours? You were only twelve."

"You don't understand. The other children mocked me, calling my mother and father cowards for leaving the Guard. I went home and yelled at my mother. I told her I was ashamed of her for deserting the Guard. We argued, and she agreed to take up her sword that very afternoon to prove she was no coward."

"And the Horde killed your mother and then your father when he went after her," Johnis said.

"I haven't stepped into a classroom since."

"I'm sorry. I'd hate to be one of the children who mocked you."

She nodded. "There were a few broken noses the next week; we'll leave it at that."

He left her alone then, not wanting to risk losing her friendship.

The first sign of pain crept into Johnis's bones when the sun was halfway down the western sky. He pulled up and flexed his fingers, surprised by how suddenly the stiffness had set in.

"The disease?" Darsal demanded, looking back at him.

"I don't know."

She lifted her arm and studied her skin. "Teeleh's teeth! So soon?"

Silvie jerked her arm up and gazed at her flesh. The tiny cracks in the skin just beneath the hair were unmistakable. Like the beginnings of a riverbed gone dry.

Johnis's heart thumped with dread. He whipped out his canteen, popped the cork, and splashed water on his forearm, eager to be free of the disease. He frantically rubbed his skin, as if washing off mulberry juice before it stained. The cracks faded.

He started to tip the canteen for more water.

"Ho, Johnis, slow down!" Silvie cried. "The horses will die before we do at this rate. Save the water for them."

He looked at her face and saw the faint cracks on her cheeks as well. But she was right—they didn't have enough water. Not bathing would make them Scabs, but not drinking would kill them and their horses. Better Horde than dead. Or was it?

"The disease affects your mind," Darsal said. "They say it turns you into an idiot. When that happens, we'll just wait for the Horde to catch us. We'll probably celebrate our defection with them!"

"I'm not willing to assume they're as foolish as we say they are," Johnis said. "They trapped us in the canyons, didn't they? Either way, we'd better hurry."

"Hurry where?" Silvie asked.

"Just hurry!"

As it turned out, hurrying didn't do them much good. It only tired the horses faster and drove them to greater desperation. The sky had turned red, the desert had flattened again, the horses were down to limping, and there was still no sign of water.

Worse, there was no longer any sign of the Horde behind them. Even the desert dwellers had given up the pursuit, probably convinced that the recruits would be doomed this deep in the desert.

Slowly, like the inching of a slug, they settled into plodding hopelessness.

Johnis stopped them when the sun dipped past the horizon. His mind was starting to go, he thought. The pain had set in so strongly that he had trouble dismounting. When he was ten he'd fallen from a mango tree, landed on his back, and rolled down a hill, over a bed of rocks, and into a stream. He'd suffered a broken collarbone and a badly bruised body. The next morning he hadn't been able to move.

This felt like that, only with fire on the skin.

"We have to rest," he said, grimacing with each step.

"If we lie down, we might never get up," Darsal said. "Maybe we should use the last of the water for a spit bath."

Silvie sat in her saddle, looking miserable. Her once-flawless face was gray and cracking already. But worse, her blue eyes had dulled and were turning white.

Johnis walked back to his horse and pulled down his blanket, shaking. "We have to rest."

Thinking that his arms hurt too much to be used as a pillow, he turned back, flipped open his saddlebag, withdrew the leather-bound Book of History that was wrapped in cloth, and dropped it at the head of his blanket.

He was happy to see that Darsal had dismounted, and now Silvie eased herself out of the saddle. They moved without speaking, plopping their blankets next to his.

One good thing, he thought, *is that we are past our bickering.* Fighting this much pain, none of them had the energy to stand, much less argue with one another.

"We should tie the horses," Silvie said.

But none of them got up to do it. One by one the three horses lay down. There was nowhere for them to go anyway.

Johnis stared out at the flat white desert, suddenly feeling like a complete fool. Or worse, a monster who'd mistaken himself for a prophet. Roush or no Roush, the very idea that they should set off into the desert to save the world was about as naive as you could get.

He lay on his blanket and stared at the flat sand. Beneath his head lay that book. There was something about that book. Oh yes, the thing about blood. Maybe using it for a pillow wasn't so brilliant, with a cut on his head and all. But it was wrapped, wasn't it? And his cut had probably stopped bleeding by now.

"Fellows—" he started, but then realized they weren't fellows. They were both girls. But they would understand. He had to set the record straight, and he didn't care whether they were fellows or girls. So he just told them what he felt.

"I've been an idiot," he said in a dry voice.

Neither disagreed, and that hurt a little. They could have said something nice, like "Don't be silly, Johnis." But they were right not to disagree. He *had* been an idiot, hadn't he?

"I don't know what got into me. Trapped in the canyon like that, with the Horde coming down on us, what did you expect? I was probably fantasizing. And now we're going to die because I fantasized two fuzzy white bats who told me to go off and save the world. I'm sorry, really. I was an idiot."

They didn't even look at him. They could at least look at him.

"Will you forgive me?" he asked, trying to ignore his self-pity.

But Silvie and Darsal just lay down on their backs and stared at the first stars, twinkling in the red sky. *It is too early to sleep,* Johnis thought, resting like a lump.

"What happens if we're Scabs when we wake?" Darsal asked.

It took a while for Silvie to answer. "Then I'll kill my first Scab," she said. "You won't mind, will you, Johnis?"

"You'll kill me?"

"I'm sworn to kill Scabs, and you'll be a Scab. I won't have a choice."

"Even if you're a Scab?"

"Does that change my vow?" she asked.

Johnis thought about that. "I suppose if I'm a Scab, I'd prefer to be dead. Go ahead, kill me."

Darsal faced him, wearing a scowl. "You see why all but the foolish understand that the legends are nothing more than ghost stories? Because pretending to see white and black bats when they don't exist can get you killed. If I live through this, I'm going to remember that."

"I'm sorry, Darsal," Johnis said, and he really was. He wasn't so sure he really had seen the Roush, or for that matter, the Shataiki bats. He had, after all, been accused of daydreaming more than once. What if it was all a mistake?

"I'm really sorry, guys."

Johnis shifted his body on the blanket. Resting his head on the book in its cloth, he closed his eyes and let his mind fade. Darsal began to snore softly.

WHAT JOHNIS DIDN'T NOTICE THROUGH THE FOG CLOUDing his mind was that the cloth had fallen free from one corner of the book.

That and the fact that he'd used his head to level Jackov two days ago. The cut on his scalp had scabbed but then broken open when he'd scratched it as his skin became diseased.

There was blood on his head.

And the book of terrible power beneath.

FIFTEEN

The valley of the Horde, deep in the western desert, lay silent in the morning light. Qurong dipped his fingers in a bowl of porridge, sucked the slop from his hand, and wiped the residue on his white bed-robe. Purple drapes divided his eating chamber from the cooking tent. Bronze statues of the winged bats called Shataiki occupied every corner—at the priest's insistence. This religion of his gave Qurong a chill, and truthfully, he didn't know why.

"Take this away," he growled. He took a swig of beer—the only drink he trusted anymore.

The cook came in with his head bowed, took the bowl off the table, and shuffled off into the adjoining room. Qurong had left Barok, his regular cook, back in the city and brought this slug, who was better fit to feed horses than humans.

The traitor had made good on his word, beginning with the insertion of spies into the forests: Horde who were forced to bathe in the lakes so that they looked like the Forest Dwellers until their mission was over and they could turn back to a more agreeable Horde state. And if they had any doubts about returning to the Horde, they would have to contend with the deaths of their families. This insurance had been the traitor's idea, and it worked well. Evidently a man's appetite for his family strengthened after bathing in the cursed lakes. Weakness, but weakness that played to Qurong's favor.

One such spy had watched the game Thomas had forced on his people—something called "football," played with a Horde-hair ball. The spy had informed them that four recruits had been sent on a mission. But he was interested only in the marked one, and then only because the traitor and that cursed priest had insisted that this one runt could play an important role in the war against the forests.

A rap sounded on the frame of his tent.

"Come."

The traitor stepped in first, followed by Tulong, the colonel he'd placed in charge of the prisoner who'd escaped during the night. The traitor preferred to wear his hood over his head at all times, in part because he was still growing his hair long enough for locks.

"You called us," Tulong said.

"What is this? You have no respect for authority?"

"Forgive me. This new order is just . . . new."

The new order he was speaking of was something the traitor had suggested, putting the army under a system not so different from the way the Forest Guard ran things.

"Yes, well, get used to it." Qurong spit. "I was told you lost our prisoner in the middle of the night. Tell me I've heard wrong."

Tulong hesitated.

"One simpleton in your grasp and he's gone?"

"Yes."

"*Sir.*"

"Yes, sir," Tulong said.

"And have you discovered who took this young fighter?"

"Not yet."

"And why not? There's no trail?"

"They dragged the body. But then the marks vanished."

"Just vanished? I would guess it's your investigative skill that has vanished."

Tulong didn't react. *His heartless demeanor makes him a good officer,* Qurong thought. *No reason to expect any feeling from him.*

"Some are saying it was magic," Tulong said.

"Bah! Magic. There is no such thing. The other three?"

"Gone into the desert. Deep."

Qurong faced the traitor, who'd remained silent. There was a mystery about him that was nearly irresistible.

"But this changes nothing," Qurong said. It came out more like a question.

"The prisoner is Horde by now," the traitor said. "But the marked one is with the others. They should never have been allowed to escape."

"They are deep in the desert. Horde as well. This means nothing."

"And why haven't they turned back to join us?"

A good question. The traitor only asked good questions. "They will," Qurong said.

"Then let's wait until they do," the traitor said. "If for no other reason than to satisfy the priest. He insists that black magic is underfoot, and the word is spreading through the army."

"What do you suggest?"

"We tell the forces that we will delay our attack until we have them. We don't need tales of black magic haunting our men when they attack the forest."

This is what makes the traitor so special, Qurong thought. *Whereas before, the Horde army has relied solely on brute force, he brings trickery and planning and double-talk to the war. A good thing.*

"How long?" he asked. "You yourself have said that we depend on surprise, which we now have on our side. If we delay, we risk the campaign."

"The Guard has massed on the eastern front, and they are digging in," the traitor said. "We attack from the opposite side as planned in two days, when they are fully entrenched."

"Good. Pass the word."

THOMAS HUNTER STOOD ON THE LEDGE, SCANNING THE canyons to his right and left. They'd come with a hundred fighters and spent the night searching with dogs, but they had found no sign that the four had reentered the forests after arriving at the Igal point.

Now, in daylight, the fighters were searching from the cliffs for any sign of the recruits.

"Anything, Mikil?" he asked.

Mikil stood atop the Igal point, using the eyeglass Thomas had formed from melted-sand glass and a hollowed gourd. "Nothing." She lowered the glass. "If they are out there, they're either Scabs or dead."

"Impossible. I'm telling you right now that we haven't found their bodies because they *escaped* the Horde."

"They might have," she said. "Or were taken prisoner. Either way, they don't have enough water to bathe. We found Billos's horse with the extra water."

"Then we go after them," Thomas said.

None of the others knew about the prophecy or the fact that Johnis was marked. Then again, there was always the possibility that the birthmark on Johnis just resembled a circle without any connection to the prophecy. If so, he'd sent a boy to his death for no good reason, an innocent boy who had no business in the Forest Guard.

William spoke on his left. "We can't risk it, not so close to a battle on the other side of the forests. Besides, you have to know that if the four recruits escaped, they would have headed back into the forests. We'd have found them by now."

"They could have gone out into the desert," Thomas said.

"Only fools would do something like that. Were they chosen for their foolishness? And if they did head out into the desert, they're dead."

William sighed and turned toward the desert. "Face it, Thomas, these four are lost to the Horde. If they're still alive, we'll fight them in battle one day. But for now we should get on with the Horde at hand. We have to return to Middle and coordinate preparations."

"I could stay with fifty men," Thomas said.

"Please, sir. The men need their commander to show strength. Their lives are at risk as much as these four. You have to go back."

Thomas knew his officer was right. Admitting it aloud wasn't so easy. If it weren't for the disease, he would mount an extended search for Johnis, Billos, Darsal, and Silvie. But by the time they organized, the four would be Scabs.

"I don't like it," Thomas said.

"There's little to like these days," William said.

A thudding of hooves crashed in from behind, and Thomas turned to see a large brown stallion bursting from the forest. In its saddle sat Ramos, Johnis's father, in full battle dress. He reined up on his horse's frothy bit.

He drilled Thomas with a hard stare.

"Dropped a cactus, is that it?"

William put his hand on the handle of his sword, but Thomas immediately motioned him back.

"I had hoped so. But wasn't willing to take the chance."

Ramos studied him, then dismounted his horse and stepped forward. "And?"

They locked stares. Thomas's heart broke for the man. "We don't know, Ramos."

"But no sign?"

"No sign."

Ramos marched to the edge and stared out at the desert canyons. "Then we go after them. We mount an expedition this moment."

"There's nothing I would like better," Thomas said. "Their water was found on a horse." He walked up and looked at the pale desert with Ramos. "Even if we left now, we wouldn't find them before the disease—"

"No!" Ramos roared, knocking Thomas's hand aside. "No! We go now. He's out there, you hear me? My boy is out there, and I will not allow him to die or turn into one of those filthy beasts!"

William walked forward. "Ramos, we are gathering for battle."

Ramos broke then, standing on the cliff next to Thomas. His red face twisted in rage, and spittle flew from his mouth with each word. "Are you all cowards?" he screamed at Thomas. "You sent him to his death! He's a boy, just a boy with a Horde ball who felt compelled by his mother's death to cross your foolish line! He doesn't deserve to be deserted!"

Thomas gently motioned William back and let the man have his emotions. "I'm sorry, Ramos. My heart breaks with yours. But the forests are at stake."

"So is my son!"

He snatched his sword in panic and started for his horse, but Thomas grabbed him by the shoulder.

"You can't go after him, Ramos."

He spun back, tears wet in his eyes. "They killed my wife! Now you say I should let them take my son?"

"And if you go after Johnis, your daughter will be without a father."

His words stopped the man cold. They all knew there was nothing one man or ten men or a hundred men could do to save one who'd gone into the desert without water. The number of men who'd lost their lives trying could hardly be counted.

Ramos's lips began to tremble. Tears leaked silently down his cheek.

"You can't find him, Ramos," Thomas said gently. "But don't give up hope. Johnis is a very special boy. This is not over, I promise you."

The man whirled around, leaped onto his horse, and spurred it toward the forest. Without a word he thundered away.

"He's a sergeant?" Thomas asked.

"Yes, sir."

"Now he's a captain," he said. "See that he gets his honors."

SIXTEEN

The three lost recruits lay in the cool desert night, snoring and occasionally groaning as disease overtook body and mind.

The body would still function well enough, but with pain and revolting smells obvious to all but those who were afflicted by it.

The mind would also function well enough, but with a limited capacity to appreciate a disease-free state of living.

Five hours into sleep, the disease had sufficiently worked its way through Johnis's skin to stretch it ever so slightly, a condition that often resulted in cracking. Fresh blood seeped from his head wound and began to snake down his hair toward the book.

All would have been fine if Johnis hadn't grunted and turned his head in the throes of some disturbing dream. But as fate would have it, when he did, his bloody locks made contact with the only part of the Book of History that wasn't covered by the cloth.

And in that moment, Johnis's world changed.

JOHNIS WAS LYING IN A FITFUL SLEEP WHEN HIS MIND exploded with black light that seared his nerves. He jerked and screamed out in pain.

He wasn't sure if the pain came from the blackness itself or from his sudden movement in the diseased state. The man-beast shrouded in black was there again, striding forward from a surreal world, reaching for him.

A moan shattered his ears, and he threw both hands over them, screaming once again.

Then the pain was gone. And the man-beast in black vanished.

Johnis wanted it all to be gone, wanted to wake up, maybe even wanted to be dead, but darkness still fogged the corners of his vision.

He could hear his breathing, long and heavy, echoing in the fuzzy tunnel ahead of him. Another image slowly came into view at the center of the foggy hole.

A desert dune. In daylight. And in fact, Johnis himself was standing at the face of the hole, part of the darkness behind him, part of the day-lit desert ahead.

He reached his hands out to feel the air, and he could swear that the air in front of him was warmer than the darkness behind. Crazy—yes, of course—but so real.

At least in his mind. Or was it more than his mind?

His horse suddenly ran down the dune directly in front of him, stepped to the right, and looked back up the dune he'd come from. To Johnis's amazement, a man stumbled over the crest of the dune, stared at him hard, and walked toward him.

The image was a bit distorted, as if heat was rising between them, but that didn't make it any less real.

This wasn't the threatening man-beast, nor Horde, but Johnis couldn't breathe anyway. Something was very wrong. The man wore a shirt made from a thin fabric, with writing across the breast, and fitted blue pants. Leather boots—but not the dress of a warrior.

More than his dress, the man's demeanor was out of place. Rather than walking like a skeleton in the desert, this man looked healthy. As if he'd had all the water he needed.

Johnis stepped back, frightened by the sight.

"Hey," the man said in a very strange accent. "What's . . ." He looked around. "What's going on?"

Johnis was too stunned to speak.

"You from Summerville?" the man demanded.

"I'm from the Middle Forest," Johnis said. "We need water."

The man eyed him carefully. "Show me the town, and I'll show you water."

"But I don't know a town out here," Johnis stammered. Perhaps the man was mad from the desert heat after all.

"The town, Summerville." The man motioned to the dune

behind him to the right. "There's a killer forcing us to play a game. I need you to help me find the cops. Tell them to get to the library. It's all about the library, tell them."

Heat shimmering off the sand distorted both the man and his words for a moment, then passed.

"Cop?" Johnis had never heard the word. It could be a code word for Horde. The Horde were in the library? "Have you seen my two friends, Silvie and Darsal?"

The man looked completely flat-footed. Maybe he'd been bitten by the desert heat, turned stupid. Johnis looked in the direction of the supposed place called Summerville. When he turned back, the man was gone.

Gone!

Johnis scanned the distorted dune, but nothing changed. He stepped back, just one step, and the hole suddenly closed in front of him, as if drawn by a noose.

Blackness filled his vision.

And the black man-beast was back, reaching—reaching and moaning. This time Johnis saw that he had more books with him, under his arm, but he couldn't tell how many because the long fingers reached for his throat, and he had to jump back or die. Yes, he knew he would die if he let those fingers/claws touch him.

Johnis screamed and opened his eyes.

Daylight blinded him, and he snapped his eyes shut. When he opened them again, he saw that he was back in the desert.

His horse was lying at his feet. Two bodies lay against him, one on each side, snoring softly. He turned his head and stared at Silvie's graying face inches from his own.

Silvie lay dead to the world, mouth parted slightly, breathing through some mucus that had gathered in her throat. He fought a sudden fit of empathy for her. Her skin was cracking and puffy. And she smelled.

Something nudged his other shoulder, and he turned to see that Darsal was nestled against his arm, faring no better. And if he could see himself in the reflection of water, he would undoubtedly see that his own skin was hanging from his bones.

"Johnis?"

Silvie had opened her eyes and was staring at him.

"Are we dead?" she asked.

Johnis pushed himself up, grimacing with pain. The horses were still alive; that was good. The Book of History lay where he'd placed it for a pillow, smudged now with a small circle of blood. He'd made a terrible mistake. *Never again,* he thought.

He picked up the book, wrapped it tightly, and shoved it back into his saddlebag. Whatever happened, he knew now that he had to protect this book at all costs.

"We have to give the stallions water," he said. "They won't make it long."

He watched Silvie struggle to her feet, amazed at the disease's progression through the night. *What have I done? I'm the supreme commander of utter fools, and now we will all pay.*

The desert rose with small dunes to the north, he saw. "Maybe they've sent out a search party." But he knew this was only more fool's talk. Better to head north, into those dunes he'd dreamed about.

Johnis was slipping the book into his saddlebag when suddenly the dots connected in his mind. Dunes to the north? Just as he'd dreamed!

His pulse suddenly pounded in his ears. "Fellows?"

They didn't even look at him.

"Girls, I think I may know where we can find water," he said.

"I hope you *drown* in your fantasies of water," Darsal rasped.

"But you see those dunes?" He pointed north. "I dreamed that those dunes were there, and I met a man who told me Summerville was there. There's water in Summerville."

Silvie moved painfully, watering her horse from her canteen, still refusing to look at him. "Fine, Johnis," she said. "Lead us to our deaths. Why stop now?"

"You'll follow me?"

"Into hell, remember?"

He gave his horse the rest of his water, then managed to mount despite his hurting flesh. "Okay, follow me."

In reality he had no clue what they'd find. Dunes, he could see that much. But the idea of water being there did seem like a fantasy.

They trudged through the desert, over the dunes. Nothing. So maybe he had been wrong.

They crested the fifth dune and pulled up.

There, in the valley below, a pond of sweet blue water shone in the rising sun, bordered by several tall palm trees and some large cacti. Catalina cacti.

"Water," Silvie said, staring dumbly.

A painful grin split Johnis's face. "Water."

SEVENTEEN

They took off, leaving Darsal gaping in their dust, then flogging her horse to catch them.

Ahead a white head poked up from the bush, then dove into the pond and disappeared.

"Did you see that?" Johnis cried. "A Roush."

"See what?"

So they still weren't seeing. But they *had* found water.

Darsal caught them before they reached the pond, and all three rolled from their horses in pain, landed on the sandy shore, and flung themselves into the glistening water.

The question now was, what kind of water? There was the drinking variety found in many streams throughout the forests, and the lake variety found in only the one lake at the center of each forest.

TED DEKKER

Was this water Elyon's?

Johnis knew the moment his skin hit the cool liquid that they had found gold. The waters of Elyon reached into his flesh, burning it like a hot iron for one terrible moment. It was no wonder the Horde feared water. He thought he could actually hear a hiss as the power spread through his skin, vaporizing the disease until the pain was gone entirely.

He sank below the surface, hardly able to contain his joy. And there, under the water, he trembled with relief.

Johnis burst from the pond, fist raised high. "Ha! What did I tell you? What did I tell you?"

"Ha!" a white Roush cried on the shore, wing jutting high like Johnis's fist.

"Gabil!"

"Johnis!"

"You're here!"

"*You're* here!"

The white bat shook its fur, spraying him with water.

The water parted as first Silvie, then Darsal, emerged facing Johnis with glowing, tanned skin and wearing impossibly wide smiles. They stared at him for a moment, then all three began to speak at once.

Johnis: "I'm sorry this happened like . . ."

Darsal: "You were right, Scrapper . . ."

Silvie: "You've yet to be wrong . . ."

They laughed like children, lost in relief and life, and for the moment they were ecstatic. Above them the sun shone in a blue sky. Below, in this oasis of living water, leafy palms swayed in a gentle breeze. Even the cacti bristling with thorns looked at peace among the gray boulders. They'd found a pocket of Elyon's power in the desert of death.

"I guess this settles it," Silvie said.

"The Horde must not get this far out," Darsal said. "If they knew this pond existed, they would have filled it in long ago."

Silvie scooped up a palmful of the water and let it dribble through her fingers. "I thought Elyon's water could only be found in the forests."

Behind her Gabil was rocking back and forth, grinning from ear to ear, bursting at the seams with an eagerness to be noticed.

"You believe me now," Johnis said. "That's what's important."

Darsal frowned, but her eyes were bright. "Do we have a choice?"

"I believe you, Johnis," Silvie said. "We're the fools, not you."

"Then maybe you should turn around and tell me what you see."

They looked over their shoulders, then jumped back as one.

Gabil crossed one wing over his chest and snapped his spindly legs together like a soldier reporting for duty. "Master Roush—defeater of the slimy, snake-eyed, putrid-breathed beasts—reporting. Otherwise known as Gabil."

"You . . . you're a Roush," Silvie stammered. Then to Johnis, "They really do exist?"

Darsal blinked. "You're a ghost?"

"Do I look like a ghost to you?" Gabil demanded.

"No. Well, you are as white as a ghost."

"But ghosts don't know karate." The white bat kicked his thin leg out from under a round torso, tried to steady himself with a flutter of wings, and toppled backward. He hopped back up, frowning. "Sorry, sorry. Not used to the air out here in this hot, very hot desert. Normally that goes much better. Do you know karate? That's what Thomas Hunter calls it in his dreams."

"You mean this?" Darsal lunged from the pond dripping wet, snapped the air with a perfect roundhouse kick above her head, and dropped into a crouch, ready to defend.

Gabil stood as tall as he could, which was just over two feet, stuck out his chest, and eyed Darsal as if trying to decide whether he approved or not. "Close enough, I guess. Although that's not perfect. One day I'll show you the finer forms of karate."

"Show me now if you—"

"No." Gabil halted her with an extended wing. "Not enough time now. Too much to do. I have a message for you."

Johnis and Silvie exchanged suppressed smiles as they stepped from the pond.

"He's so cute," Silvie whispered.

Gabil's ears perked immediately. "What's that? Am I?"

She knelt on one knee and kissed him on the forehead. "The cutest creature I've ever dreamed to meet."

Johnis couldn't tell if Gabil turned red under his white fur, but he was clearly smitten by Silvie's generous praise. Or perhaps more by her. He paced unsteadily and stroked his chin, acting the part of importance.

"Well, I've never been called cute. A mighty fighter, an expert flyer, a defender of the land, the greatest Roush who ever did terrify Teeleh, but never cute. I'll take it as a compliment." He bowed.

But Johnis knew that Gabil would rather be cute, as Silvie put it, than anything. She'd won his loyalty for life.

The Roush cleared his throat. "Now the message Michal sent me to deliver is this: This water"—he pointed at the pond—"is the water you were looking for."

They stood dripping around him. "That's it?" Darsal said.

"That's not important?"

"We already know this is water."

"Well, it's not my fault that I waited two days here, baking in this blasted heat while you bickered away the hours in the desert. But you've made it. You're the first humans to ever lay eyes on this pool."

Gabil glanced at the horizon. "I really should be going. I wasn't technically supposed to . . . you know . . . swim with you. Just keeping an eye out. That's all I'm doing." He sauntered away from the pool.

"Now what?" Darsal asked.

Gabil looked back at her. "He didn't tell you?"

"Well, he said something about the six lost Books of—"

"Then you know. Did he also tell you that he would die?"

She glanced at Johnis.

"Then again, all humans die," Gabil said. "Sooner or later. Sooner if you make mistakes."

He stared at them, then suddenly jumped up, swung one spindly leg around in a roundhouse kick similar to the one executed by Darsal, and landed with a *Hayaa!*

A sly smile split his face. "You like that? That's how a real karate kick is done. And next time I'll show you even more."

He waited, expecting an encouraging response, so Silvie gave him one. "That's good, Gabil. We look forward to it."

"I knew it," he said. "I told Michal you would need my help!"

He leaped into the air and swooped over the sand. He'd gone a hundred yards before circling back and yelling down at them, "The rock, look at the rock!"

And then he was gone.

Johnis looked around. "Rock?"

"Rock," Silvie said, walking to a large, angular stone with a flat top jutting from the sand beside the pond. "This rock."

They stood over it together, staring at words that looked as if they'd been etched into the surface a hundred years ago.

Beyond the blue another world is opened.
Enter if you dare.
In the west, the Dark One seeks seven
To destroy the world.

A shiver passed through Johnis as he read the words. "'Beyond the blue'?"

"A path," Silvie said. "To the Dark One."

Darsal stepped around the rock, studying the words. "I don't like it."

"I don't think it really matters if you like it," Johnis said. "We're not here by accident."

Silvie was still contemplating the riddle. "'Beyond the blue?' The sky's blue."

"So is the water," Johnis said.

"It also says 'Enter if you dare,'" Darsal said. "That doesn't sound like an order to me. We have a choice."

Johnis walked to the edge of the water, knelt down, and stared into the mirrored surface. His face looked back at him, smooth and tanned again. He impulsively closed his eyes and lowered his head into the pool. With no disease to heal, the cool water felt like nothing more than a pool of water, so he pulled himself out.

"Anything?" Silvie asked.

"Nothing."

She knelt beside him, watching her reflection as the pool stilled again. "Did you open your eyes?"

"No."

She stuck her face into the water, was still for a moment, then suddenly jerked it out, gasping.

"What?"

"Eyes of Elyon, it's . . . There's something inside!"

Without waiting to hear any further explanation, Johnis and Darsal both plunged their heads underwater.

The deep pool below exploded with light. The light vanished as quickly as it had appeared, but now something else filled Johnis's vision: a black void, and at the center of that void a single Book of History, crackling with light, as if the light was trying to get out.

The book was now joined by another and another and four more until there were seven—one black, one brown, one blue, one green, one purple, one red, and one more Johnis couldn't make out because it was covered by the others. All seven became one book, and the red twine vanished, absorbed by the covers.

The shrouded black man-beast with long claws suddenly stepped in and sank his nails into the book. He tried to pry it open. Arcs of lightning shot from the pages, struck Johnis in the face, and shook him to his bones.

He jerked his head out of the water, gasping. Silvie and Darsal both had their heads in the pool, but they came up, too, hollering in pain.

For a few moments they just stared at one another. Then back at the water, stunned by the power.

"It's like another world," Silvie breathed.

"'In the west, the Dark One seeks Seven,'" Johnis said. "The seven Books of History."

Darsal stood and wiped at the water on her face. "I don't like it."

"We have to go west," Johnis cried. "We have to keep the seven books from the Dark One."

"And do we even know who the Dark One is?"

"Teeleh. It has to be."

"The Roush are one thing," Darsal said. "Maybe even Shataiki. But are you sure this mythical creature named Teeleh truly exists? Besides, the Roush saved us from death. Surely you're not suggesting we continue on west, further into this blasted desert that not even the Horde will inhabit."

"I am."

"We can't!"

Silvie walked to her horse, who'd filled its belly with water. She pulled out her canteen and returned to the pond.

"What are you doing?" Darsal demanded.

"Preparing for the journey," she said.

Darsal drilled Johnis with a hard stare. "That's right. We have plenty of water for the journey home, Scrapper. I suggest you fill your canteen as well."

"The journey west," Silvie said. She stood and plugged the leather bottle she'd filled with a cork. "I'm with Johnis. It's true, Darsal. Everything he's told us is true."

"And I'll tell you what else is true. Billos is gone, captured by the Horde. The disease has probably turned him into a Scab. We have to find him, and that means a rescue mission with veteran fighters. Now that we have water, we have to go back for help— for Billos's sake if for no other reason!"

"Even if we did go back," Johnis said, "we couldn't tell Thomas what we've learned."

"Why not?"

"Because the Roush ordered us not to."

"You're putting too much stock in a white bat who thinks he knows how to fight. I could never break my vow to the supreme commander by keeping all this hidden."

"For the love of Elyon," Johnis said, "you've just learned that the legends are all real and you still question this calling?"

Darsal looked to the desert, frowning. "I don't know what I'm questioning. None of this feels right. And they have Billos! He should be here, bathing in this water."

Johnis stared at her for a long time, trying to think of how to help her see the light. But perhaps there were secrets in her heart that were making her as stubborn as a log. And he didn't think Michal had intended for him to be her parent.

"Then we should split up," he finally said. "We go on, you head back. Is that what you want?"

Darsal marched to her horse, face red. "That's fine by me. But don't say I didn't warn you. I know what I saw in the pool."

"What did you see?" Silvie asked.

She turned back. "I saw death." Then she added as an after-thought, "Both of you are going straight down into hell."

EIGHTEEN

Freshly watered and fed, the horses struck out with surprising willingness. But the desert heat quickly reminded Johnis and Silvie that their water would only last so long. They made note of the oasis's location between distant dunes and the sun. Looking at the white flats stretching west, Silvie suggested that maybe Darsal had been right in suggesting they were headed straight down to hell.

But both agreed that Darsal would eventually come to her senses and realize that going back alone presented just as many challenges as going on did. For one thing, the Horde was behind them—reaching the forests wouldn't be an easy thing. And she could just as easily get lost as be taken by the Horde. Silvie said she expected Darsal to gallop up behind them at any moment.

But that moment never came.

They headed due west, and except for the sun rising and falling over their heads, nothing changed. The desert remained flat and hot. The horses plodded forward, always forward.

Silvie and Johnis talked as their horses walked. It was all they could do. And for Johnis it was more than enough, learning what Silvie loved and hated about life—slowly uncovering the heart that hid beneath layers of skin.

She loved peanuts, which she scolded him for not bringing. The sago palm cakes he'd brought weren't fit for horses, much less humans, she claimed. Although when he gave her one he'd salted with black rock salt from the Southern Forest, she ate the whole thing without complaining.

She preferred wearing red flowers in her hair because her mother wore red. Elisa, her mother, had been nothing short of a miraculous woman, she said. And then she spent an hour explaining exactly why.

When it came to weapons, Silvie preferred a knife to a sword because she'd learned how to throw them from a good distance. With a sword you had to get in close, she said. She showed Johnis how to throw one of the four she carried and was impressed by his quick learning. A natural, she said. Unusual.

They talked about a hundred things, and all the while Johnis became more and more aware that they were slowly but surely abandoning themselves to this unexplored desert. An afternoon wind scattered their tracks, making it impossible to retrace them.

"Have you ever fallen in love?" Johnis asked as the afternoon turned red.

Silvie looked at him and winked. "Once. When I was fifteen. You?"

Talk of love was common and encouraged among the Forest Dwellers. Their religion, the Great Romance, had started when Tanis, the firstborn, had given his love to Teeleh, they said. Now the greatest reminder of Elyon's love was found between a man and a woman, though a father or mother's love for a child came a close second.

"Yes," Johnis said. "I loved a girl named Mirim last year. She was a very . . . nice girl."

"Was she? But you no longer love her?"

"My father says that I'm too young to really know love. Maybe he's right."

"Bah! Don't you believe it," she said. "If you're old enough to die in battle, you're old enough to understand the love you die for."

Johnis nodded. "The love of Elyon. But that's not the same."

"No? That's not what the elders teach. It may not have always been like this, but when we fight for our lives, we should also be allowed to love for our lives."

"So then, do you love this boy of yours?" he asked.

"I do."

Johnis felt his heart sink. She was in love with another boy? He realized then how much hope he'd unconsciously put in her.

"Well, that's nice."

"It is and it isn't," she said. Then she winked at him again, and Johnis cursed his heart for its impulsive leap. He didn't have the time or the mind or the heart to love a woman at this moment. He was committing himself to death, for the sake of Elyon.

"You're disappointed?" she asked with a smile.

"Why should I be? He must be a very happy boy."

"Hmmm."

"Hmmm?" he repeated. "What does that mean?"

"I was rather hoping you'd be disappointed. It's always nice to be loved."

Johnis didn't know what to make of that. Women could be quite crafty, he knew that much. His father said it often. Smarter than men, too, most of the time. You had to know your way around if you wanted to fall in love with a woman. *"Best to wait, lad. Just take your time. No rush."*

"It is nice, isn't it?" he said. Their eyes met, and he blushed a little.

The sun dipped over the horizon an hour later, and all notions of love vanished with it. Johnis pulled up. For a long while they stared at the growing darkness in silence.

"What if the desert never ends?" Silvie wondered aloud. She sounded as if she was doubting again.

"We should keep moving while the sun is down," he said. "The disease will begin again tomorrow."

"I agree," she said. "It's so"—she looked around and shivered—"quiet out here."

"We can talk," Johnis said.

Silvie started her horse forward again. "I would like that."

But they went for ten minutes without talking.

"Johnis?"

"Yes?"

"I'm scared."

"I know. I am too."

DARSAL SAT ON THE DUNE, FACING EAST, TRYING TO DECIDE if that really was dead east or just sort of east. Because if it wasn't dead east, she could easily miss the entire forest, and that would guarantee her death.

She knew the stars well enough, but she'd never had to navigate by them. A few inches one way or the other could mean many miles farther on. She knew the sun better, and she thought it might be smarter to wait until morning. The last thing she wanted to do was run into a Horde camp.

On the other hand, she still had an awful long way to go, and the disease wouldn't wait. The sooner she got to the forest, the greater the likelihood of her survival.

And the sooner she could apply herself to finding Billos. Thoughts of what might have happened to him sent shivers of fear down her spine.

Her horse gave off a terrified bray behind her, and she spun around to see that it was forty yards off, lying on the ground. And it wasn't just a matter of being tired.

There was blood on the sand by its belly.

Blood?

Darsal's heart slammed into her throat. The animal's skin quivered for several long seconds, then stilled. Someone had just killed her horse!

She stood frozen to the sand. Her sword was under the beast, pinned to the ground. Without a horse, without a sword, she was lost.

Something made a soft brushing sound behind her where she knew nothing but dunes lay. Slowly, terrified of what she might find, Darsal turned around.

There on the sand, in a wide half-circle starting to her right and extending all the way around to her left, stood a throng of black bats, staring at her with beady red eyes. Hundreds, maybe thousands.

Their wings hung to the sand—this was the brushing sound she'd heard. Their jaws were open, all of them, revealing dirty fangs and mucus. And then they stepped toward her, like a slow tide, eyes unmoving.

Darsal ripped her feet from the ground, whirled around, and tore into the night, screaming in mindless terror. She knew it was hopeless, but she didn't expect what came next.

One of them, maybe more, slammed into her back and sent her flying onto her face. They were on her before she could even scramble to her knees. Fangs sank into her forearms and calves.

Her hair and clothing were jerked up, and she was lifted from the desert floor, still facedown. Wind from their wings beat against her face. They were airborne.

Or she was dead and drifting to the skies—she didn't know which. A fuzzy snout nuzzled her neck and cheek, breathing hot, foul breath over her skin.

A long scream from her own throat cut through the sounds of a thousand beating wings.

It was the last thing she remembered.

NINETEEN

Johnis and Silvie had gone for another six hours in the darkness until they were practically falling from their horses, and then they'd crashed on the sand, side by side.

Johnis dreamed of the fuzzy white bat swinging his leg in a karate kick and toppling backward in the sand. And of the blue waters in the pond, soothing his burning skin. And of Silvie kissing him. He wasn't sure why he was letting her kiss him, but he was. And he wasn't minding it.

"Johnisssssss," she whispered in his ear. He liked the sound of that. "Johnisssss." Her hand shook him. "Johnis!"

His eyes snapped open. It was still dark, and Silvie was leaning over him. Her eyes were staring into the dark past his feet.

"Wake up!" she whispered.

Johnis sat up and followed her stare. A line of red swept the horizon from north to south, like a long string.

"What is it?" she asked. "What's making that red light?"

He pushed himself to his knees. "Shataiki."

Her fingers dug into his shoulder. "Shataiki?"

Johnis hadn't seen any since leaving the canyons. Well, they were back. They sat on the ground unmoving, unblinking, far away. Just staring in perfect silence.

"Shataiki," he said again.

"What are they doing?"

"I don't know."

"What are we doing?"

"I don't know."

"Stop sounding so casual about it!"

"I . . ." But he didn't know what to say. He was terrified, sure he was. But what could he say? They had arrived.

"Where are we?" Silvie asked.

That was the question, wasn't it? Why weren't the bats attacking, or at least making a fuss? They looked as though they were guarding something rather than massing for an assault.

Johnis slowly stood to his feet. "I have this feeling."

"This doesn't look good," she said in a thin voice. "What are we supposed to do? They know we're here!"

"Yes, they do."

Silvie looked at him. "Don't tell me you're thinking what I think you're thinking."

"I have this feeling that we've made it," he said. "This is it."

"You can't be serious, Johnis. There's way too many. There's no way we came here to be killed by Shataiki bats."

The horizon had started to gray. Dawn was coming.

"I don't think we'll have to kill any of them."

Johnis walked to his horse, took a drink of water, his eyes still fixed on the beasts, and then mounted. "Drink, Silvie. We're going to need it."

"What are you doing?"

"Thinking with my heart," he said. "Thomas insisted."

"Nonsense." But she already had her canteen out. "I don't like this, Johnis. Please don't tell me you're going up there."

"Do you want to wait here?"

"No! I'm not staying alone."

"Then mount up."

She did, but not without more objections, all of which he ignored. They turned the horses due west toward the line of Shataiki. The dull morning light now revealed something else. The ground beyond the line of black bats was dark. There was more to this than met their eyes at the moment.

"Ready?"

"No," she said.

But Johnis was already moving. Forward. Toward whatever destiny awaited him two hundred yards ahead.

Slowly the shapes of the Shataiki came into focus. Vampire bats half Johnis's height, wings draping, jaws open, drooling. Like hounds fixed on their prey, unconcerned. Squatting in a line on the sand.

But Johnis was now more concerned with what lay beyond the bats than the Shataiki themselves. If they wanted to kill him and Silvie, they could have done it while they slept. Something else was happening here.

"That's a valley," Silvie whispered. "It's black."

She was right. The desert floor fell away into some kind of valley beyond the Shataiki. The bats were actually perched on the lip of a huge black bowl, extending as far as Johnis could see.

"What do you think it is?"

Surprisingly, Johnis knew what it was. "It's where the Dark One lives."

"Then it's where we'll die," Silvie said. "I wasn't quite this serious when I said I'd follow you to hell."

Johnis stopped twenty paces from the line of bats. They still stared at him, making no threats. But the fact that they sat unblinking while flies crawled on their faces seemed to be its own kind of threat.

Gray dawn now showed them what lay in the valley behind. It was a forest. Black trees. A black forest.

The legends of old crashed through Johnis's mind. How Teeleh had led the Shataiki from the Black Forest into the unspoiled colored forest, turning it to ash as he passed. That was how the desert had been formed, how evil had ravaged the land and turned a once loving, peaceful people into the Horde.

This valley was the original Black Forest?

"If we go in there, we'll never get out," Silvie said.

"Do you have any other suggestions?"

She thought about it for a long time. "No. But we can't go into that valley. Are you sure the books are in there?"

"I sure hope so." Johnis nudged his horse. It snorted and tried to turn back, but he forced it forward.

Still the Shataiki did not move.

He slapped the horse's hide. "Move!"

A single Shataiki leaped to the air thirty yards down the line and swept into the valley on black, leathery wings. But none of the others moved.

"Please, let's go back and talk this through, Johnis," Silvie said. "It doesn't feel right to me. You're not the only one committing yourself to this madness. We have to go back!"

"We can't. We came for this."

"Curse your impulsiveness, Johnis!"

He faced her, holding his jittery horse firm. "You have to trust me, Silvie. I can't blame you for not wanting to, but I need you to trust me. I was *born* for this!"

"I wasn't."

"You do know that it was these Shataiki that killed your mother and father, don't you? They probably control the Horde. I promise you, if you follow me you'll have your chance to kill more Shataiki bats than you thought possible."

She looked at the beasts. "They don't look like they would be easy to kill."

"You're magic with the knives and quick with the sword. Trust me. Please."

"Look at their claws. This is just absurd—it's two against a thousand!"

"They won't fight us. Trust me."

Her jaw flexed, but she didn't object. "They aren't going to let us pass," she said.

Johnis reached behind, withdrew the Book of History from his saddlebag, and faced the Shataiki.

Their response was immediate. First shuffling and hissing as the book came out. Then they parted in front of him, dragging their wings behind, red eyes never leaving the book.

"They are now," Johnis said.

He looked past them and saw that a bridge made from a patchwork of wood planks and poles stretched between the lip of this depression all the way to the floor, at least a hundred yards down. It was as if a giant had put his massive boot into the earth here, shoving the ground down deep. Black trees had found a way to grow at the bottom.

But there was more than trees down there. Much more. The question was, what?

He nudged his horse. It refused to budge, so he kicked it hard. With a snort of protest, the black stallion took its first step toward the Black Forest.

TWENTY

The narrow bridge creaked and groaned as Johnis and Silvie guided their horses down into the abyss. There was no railing, and the drop on either side fell a hundred yards down to bare slate rock. A fall would kill them.

Johnis glanced back at Silvie, who gripped her reins with white knuckles. Her face glistened with sweat despite the cool morning air.

"You okay?"

She shot him a frightened look, then glanced over his shoulder at the trees below. "Neither of us is okay," she said.

Behind her the Shataiki had turned around and were staring at them from the top of the cliff, content to let them descend into their world.

Johnis turned back and studied the Black Forest, searching for anything that might give him a clue as to what he was meant to do. Find the missing books, but how? For that matter, what made him think he was meant to enter this forest? Even if he did survive long enough to find the books, getting out looked to be impossible.

He gripped the book in one hand and moved his horse farther down.

It took them five minutes to reach the bottom, but those few minutes felt like an hour. Charcoal gray stone led from the bridge up to lumpy black ground from which the trees grew. Tall black angular trees without leaves. Black moss hung from the bare branches, and what looked like nests made from this moss were nestled in the crooks of the branches.

The nests undoubtedly belonged to the Shataiki watching them from the bowl's lip. A suffocating stench filled the air, so thick Johnis thought he could feel it. He shivered as they stepped off the bridge to the forest floor.

"Now what?" Silvie asked in barely more than a whisper.

"We go in," he said, nodding at the trail that cut into the forest ahead of them.

"You've lost your peanuts."

"I know. I'm following my heart, not my mind," he said. "Isn't that what Thomas told us to do?"

"I doubt he had suicide in mind. And why do you suppose there's a trail on the ground? These bat-beasts fly, right?" She paused. "Do you have *any* idea what you're doing, or are you just leading us into the jaws of death for the joy of it?"

"I don't know," he said.

"That's a problem, Johnis. This isn't a time not to know."

"All I know is that we were meant to go directly west, and this is directly west. And I know that I can't pretend I wasn't told to go directly west. I thought you agreed."

"I did agree to go directly west. But not to enter this pit of misery when we got there."

"Yet you're still following me," he said.

They walked their horses right to the forest's edge. Then under the first few moss-covered branches. Then deep into the shadows. The cliffs behind them disappeared. The Shataiki let them march ahead, content to watch from the cliff. There was evidently no need to guard trespassers who'd already committed themselves to the pit of death.

Johnis put his hand up to stop them, dropped from his mount, and handed Silvie his reins. "Wait here."

"Where are you going?"

"We're not the only ones who want this," he said, tucking the Book of History under his arm.

He hurried into the forest, counting trees. One, two, three, four, five, six, seven. He scanned the trees above him—no Shataiki that he could see—then he kicked at the ground, which was covered in ash and moss. He set the book in the hole he'd made and quickly covered it with moss. Satisfied that it looked pretty much untouched, he hurried back to where Silvie waited.

"Forty-nine trees in, seven trees south," he said, swinging back into his saddle. "You and I are the only ones who know."

Johnis wondered if he'd made a mistake telling her where he'd hidden the book. But if he couldn't trust Silvie, he could trust no one.

The first Shataiki didn't show up in the trees for another half hour; then they made themselves known with flapping and hissing high above. If Johnis wasn't mistaken, some whispering was mixed in with that hissing. These beasts could speak.

The farther in they went, the thicker the trees grew and the darker it became. They'd grown accustomed to the smell, but the thought of this putrid air working its way into their lungs made Johnis nauseated.

"How far are we going?" Silvie asked in a thin voice.

He looked at her and saw that she'd resigned herself to following him. Truth be told, *he* wasn't sure he could be trusted, but they were committed now. From the beginning of this whole mess, since battling over the Horde football, he'd trusted his instincts, moving when and where his gut told him to move. So he would continue doing the same.

But look where it had gotten him! Elyon help him. They could use Billos and Darsal now.

"'In the west, the Dark One seeks Seven to destroy the world,'" Johnis said, recalling the inscription on the stone. He looked up at a bat that swooped down and then shot back into the canopy, screeching. "We're here because the Dark One lives here."

"And he's seeking the six missing books," Silvie said. "So we go until we find this Dark One."

"Teeleh."

She set her jaw and stared ahead. "The worst he can do is kill us, right?"

"No, the worst he can do is get his claws on the seven books." He raised his voice. "That's why we're here, and that's why I hid the other book in the desert."

She blinked.

If the bats could whisper, they could listen, which was why he'd been careful not to say much. Thinking about it, he wished he *had* hidden the book in the desert, but it was too late for that now.

A long lonely scream drifted through air, and Johnis pulled up. The Shataiki scattered like a flock of parrots, squawking noisily.

"That sounded like . . ." But Silvie didn't finish.

"Like what?"

She moved ahead of him, ears tuned, and Johnis followed. Her sudden display of courage made him proud. She was, after all, the better fighter here, without contest. Silvie was his protector.

They'd gone another fifty paces when the scream came again, long and forlorn, like a thin horn blown for a funeral. The path forked in front of them, one trail veering left and one veering right, toward the sound of the cry.

"Which way?" Silvie asked.

"To the right," he said.

So she steered her horse right. The next time the scream came, it was so loud that Silvie gasped. The sound of a whip split the air. *Crack!*

Silvie twisted in her saddle, her face white with panic. "That's human!"

She suddenly kneed her horse and took off, galloping through the trees.

"Silvie!"

But she was gone, and Johnis slapped his horse into a full run after her.

The scream echoed through the forest again. And not just any scream, but one that sounded amplified and inhuman. Johnis's heart hammered with the pounding of his horse's hooves.

It was one thing to be leading, forcing himself to be confident. But following Silvie, Johnis was suddenly terrified. *We're galloping into hell,* he thought. *We've lost our minds!*

Their trip into the Black Forest stopped when the path abruptly ended at the edge of a huge hole that fell fifty feet, flattened at the bottom, then rose on the far side.

Johnis had seen this before. It was an amphitheater, nearly identical to the stadium they'd played Horde football in several days ago in the forest.

Black trees rimmed the stadium but had been cleared from the field at the bottom of the bowl. Bleachers cut from darkened slabs of rock stepped up from the field, a hundred rows at least. The field itself was made of lump ash.

At the center of the field was a pond. And next to the pond, a platform made of the black wood from these dark, angular trees.

And on the platform, a large circular wheel standing tall.

Two humans were strapped to the wheel, arms and legs spread like an X.

"Billos!" Silvie whispered.

"And Darsal," Johnis said.

Not another creature in sight.

For a few moments Johnis and Silvie were so shocked at finding their comrades alive, here in this vile forest, that they could only stare.

Darsal sagged in her ropes, limp or dead to the world. Billos's head hung to one side, but his legs twitched now and then as if they were being pricked by some unseen needle. They were stripped to the tunics they wore under their battle dress to keep the armor from chafing their skin.

Without any obvious cause, Billos suddenly arched his back, jerked his head up, and screamed with terrible pain. The sound echoed in the stadium, which amplified it and sent the scream skyward like a warning to all who could hear.

Or like an invitation to the foolish, Johnis thought.

Come and die with us, you fools. Come and join us in our pain that you cannot see.

TWENTY-ONE

Silvie jerked her horse left and right, searching for a way down to the floor of the amphitheater. "He's alive!"

Johnis wanted to stop her, wanted to tell her that Billos and Darsal surely weren't alone down there. But now she was moving by impulse, just as he had for days.

There was no path leading down to the field, only these benches cut from the black rock. Silvie slapped her horse on the rump and took it over the edge, leaning back to keep her balance. The stallion was sure-footed and trained for battle—it might shy from the stench of the Black Forest, but it didn't hesitate now.

Johnis clenched his jaw and followed, bucking with the horse as it went.

Billos was whimpering as they raced across the stadium flat

toward the pond. The wheel on which their friends were strapped stood on the platform ahead.

Shadows moved on the ground as if a cloud were moving overhead. But it wasn't a cloud, Johnis saw.

It was Shataiki bats. Thousands and thousands, flowing into the bleachers from the sky on all sides. The sight was so strange, so frightening, that he almost overshot the pond. He slid to a stop next to Silvie, and they dropped to the ground together.

In three long bounds they reached the platform, which stood three feet from the ground, like a dock on the pond's edge. One more leap and they both landed on the wood floor, crouched.

Billos and Darsal hung like rags on the large solid wheel. Their chests rose and fell in ragged breathing. Alive, but beaten and bloody from a dozen cuts or bites. The Scab disease covered their flesh. If Johnis didn't know that only Billos and Darsal could possibly be here, strapped up to die, he might not have recognized them for all the cracking and graying of their skin.

Around them the Shataiki bats continued to fill the stadium, like a wall of black fur with red beads sewn on, hissing and clicking like a million insects.

Johnis felt his heart slamming against his ribs, but he couldn't hear it for the sound of the bats. Silvie gripped her sword tightly. Johnis had forgotten his in the scabbard.

"Billos!" Silvie whispered. She started forward.

"Wait," Johnis breathed. Then louder so she could hear. "Silvie, it's a trap."

No surprise on her face. She knew already. But she was too fix-ated on easing their pain.

A thin, flea-bitten rag of a bat flapped up from his hiding place behind the wheel and streaked to the sky. He had been hurting Billos's back with the needle in his claw.

Furious at this obscene torture, Silvie screamed after the Shataiki and drew back her blade to slash the ropes that bound Billos and Darsal to the wheel. With a grunt she swung and cut one thick cord.

Billos's left arm dropped free, and his shoulder slumped for-ward. But he was unconscious now and made no effort to right himself.

Silvie drew back for a second swing, and the stadium suddenly hushed, as if she herself had signaled immediate silence. She glanced at Johnis, shifted her eyes over his shoulder, and froze, eyes wide.

Johnis felt the Dark One's presence before he saw him. An oppressive, thick blanket that robbed him of breath was approach-ing from behind.

Johnis fought a bout of panic and turned slowly. A large vam-pire beast floated in on oily black wings, huge talons extending down twice the length of his torso, which was three times the size of the other Shataiki. His mouth was a cross between a bat's snout and a wolf's jaws. Bloodred eyes bulged below a jutting brow.

This was Teeleh.

Johnis felt his stomach tighten in protest, and for a moment he thought he might throw up. He clenched his fists and stepped back, but inside he felt like water.

The beast landed on the wood with a clacking of talons. He folded his leathery wings, extended his chin, opened his jaws wide so that Johnis could see the back of his throat, and swallowed a small rodent lodged in his teeth.

"Thank you for coming," he said, his voice low and raspy.

For a long time he just stared at them, but it was hard to see where he was looking because his red eyes had no pupils.

"I can see that you're both ill," he said. "We could help you."

"They're ill," Johnis said, looking at Billos and Darsal.

"No, they're perfectly fine now. But you . . . You have a skin disease. The smell is sickening."

The beasts thought *humans* smelled? Their minds were a twisted mess.

"It's not I who see things wrong, my friend," Teeleh said. "It's you."

If the beast can read my thoughts, we're dead, Johnis thought.

Teeleh took three slow steps toward Darsal and drew a finger gently down her side, tearing the sleeve of her tunic with his razor-sharp claw.

"The human is so sickening, you know," he said, facing Johnis and Silvie. "But it won't last long. The Horde will end this madness." The Shataiki twisted his head. "The Horde. They've embraced the new world. They listen to reason."

"They wage war on the Forest Dwellers who love Elyon," Johnis said.

The creature's jaws snapped impossibly wide, and he roared with enough power to shake the platform. Hot, rancid breath blasted over Johnis, who found he couldn't move, much less jerk back, at the bat's sudden roar. Teeleh was reacting to the name Elyon?

As quickly as the roar began, it ended with a snapping of the bat's jaws. Saliva dripped over his lips and strung to the ground.

"Elyon," Johnis said.

The bat's furry, flea-bitten skin quivered. But this time he just stared.

"Do you have my book?" Teeleh asked in a grating voice.

"What book?"

"The book that makes everything right."

"The question is, do you have *my* books?" Johnis asked.

The throngs of Shataiki bats were glued to the scene. They hissed, bickered, screeched. Silvie glanced at him with questioning eyes.

Teeleh whipped his head toward his legions and snarled. Like a crackling rifle shot, the sound from his mouth echoed around the stadium, silencing them immediately.

Teeleh gathered himself. "Do you doubt my intent to have the books?"

Johnis felt his knees quake, and he tried to still them. "No."

"Do you think you can stop me?" Teeleh asked.

He answered honestly. "No."

"But you're sick with delusions about your destiny, so you can't tell me where the book is. Let me put your mind at ease. Look at your hand."

Johnis lifted his arm and saw that the flaking of his skin had already begun. So soon? It must be the Black Forest.

Teeleh's voice was low. "Humans all have the same destiny: to become Horde and to serve me. It can come easily, or it can come with great suffering. The choice is yours. In the end you will never stop me."

"Why do you need the Books of History?" Silvie asked, her voice thin.

At first Johnis wasn't sure Teeleh would answer. "To heal me," the beast said.

"You're sick?"

"I'm . . . incomplete. But I can be beautiful again." He swept his sinewy arm wide. "This can all be beautiful—if I have the books."

"I'm sorry," Johnis said. "You'll have to find another way. Maybe the Horde can help you."

Again the throng hissed their shock at his courage.

Teeleh kept his eyes fixed on Johnis and curled a single claw as a sign. Two mangy bats *whooshed* to where the horses sat, dumped the saddlebag contents unceremoniously on the ground, and began to search for the Book of History.

Eight more Shataiki flew in from behind the platform, settled to the floor around the wheel that held Billos and Darsal, and began to push the contraption forward as if it were an upended table being scooted on edge, rather than rolling it on its side.

Johnis watched in amazement as the wheel slid along the platform and out over the water on a railing system connected to a frame behind it. There was a hole in the back. The Shataiki had been stabbing Billos and Darsal with needles through that hole.

The bats spun the wheel back so that Billos and Darsal faced them again, then slapped them both until they stirred to consciousness.

They looked around with gray eyes. Darsal was the first to recognize them.

"Silvie?"

"Where?" Billos asked. "You see Silvie?"

Darsal's face wrinkled in anguish. "Oh, Silvie. I'm sorry. I'm so sorry. I shouldn't have left you."

"Is that you, Scrapper?" Billos asked, staring at Johnis. "You've come to die with us, is that it?"

"It's okay, Billos," Johnis said. "Everything will be okay."

The Shataiki cranked the wheel, turning it so that Billos and Darsal were both held parallel to the lake below them. What were they doing? They cranked again until Billos and Darsal were upside down, heads pointed at the water.

It all clicked for Johnis then. "This is a mockery of Elyon's water," he said. "He's going to drown them!"

As if on cue, one of the bats turned a large wooden handle, and the entire wheel began to descend toward the water. Their heads would go under first, Johnis realized. They would drown!

"You can't do this!" Silvie cried.

Teeleh didn't flinch.

The bottom of the wheel broke the surface and continued its descent.

"You can't kill them!" Silvie screamed, springing toward Teeleh with her sword lifted.

Moving faster than Johnis thought possible, the large vampire bat reached out with one wing and swatted Silvie to the ground as if she were nothing more than a fly. Her sword clattered on the wood planks.

Johnis stared at Billos terrified that he might actually be drowned here on account of him!

Darsal's hair slipped into the water. Then her forehead. Then Billos's hair. They didn't realize until that moment what was happening, but when they did, they both began to struggle. Their wails of desperation cut Johnis as if they were blades.

Then they were under and drowning.

Johnis threw out his arm to stop them. "Stop it!"

"Let them drown," Teeleh snarled.

"No!" Johnis scrambled for reason. "I'll give you my book! Pull them up!"

"Where is the book?" Teeleh asked, unconcerned.

"I'll tell you. Just pull them up, for the sake of Elyon!"

Teeleh might have roared with rage at the use of the name, but he seemed beyond that at the moment. He stared at Johnis, snout quivering.

"If you kill them you might as well kill me too," Johnis said, biting off each word with conviction.

Teeleh studied him as if trying to determine his true intention. If Johnis was willing to die rather than tell Teeleh the book's location, Teeleh would be lost. And Johnis was now certain he would do just that—if the beast killed Billos and Darsal, he would refuse to give up the location, no matter what else happened.

Teeleh steadied himself and nodded. The Shataiki immediately cranked the wheel, pulling Billos and Darsal from the water. The two recruits sputtered and gasped for breath.

"Well?" Teeleh said.

Johnis shook his head. "No, turn them right side up."

The black bats looked at Teeleh, saw some signal that Johnis missed, and turned the wheel right side up. Water drained from Billos and Darsal's tattered tunics and splashed into the water at their feet.

"Now let them go," Johnis said.

"Am I a fool?" Teeleh growled.

"I don't know, are you? Let these three go, and you'll have me."

"I already have you."

"And you'll get nothing from me," he cried. "It was me who got them in this mess. I'll get them out by giving you the book, but they get out first. All the way out, into the desert."

The stadium echoed with his last words, then fell quiet.

"Are you going to die with us, Scrapper?" Billos asked. He'd lost his mind to the disease, Johnis realized.

Darsal wasn't so far gone. She looked at Silvie and started to cry. "I'm sorry, Silvie. I'm so sorry."

Silvie hurried to Johnis's side, eyes flashing with fear. "You can't do this," she breathed. "Once you tell him, he'll kill you. What do you think you're doing?"

"Thinking with my heart," he said. "Is it better for all of us to die?"

Her eyes brimmed with tears. Blue eyes, just starting to gray. He leaned forward and kissed her lightly on the cheek. "Take the book with you," he whispered in her ear. "And when you reach the top of the cliff, blow your horn."

All Forest Guard carried thin horns made from the gourd reed, which, when blown, carried for miles on the still air. Silvie's was still under her belt.

Then he pulled back and faced Teeleh. "Do we have a deal?"

"Even if we do," the beast said, "how do I know you'll keep your end?"

"You don't have a choice. If you don't let them go, you'll never see the book. Kill us all, and the location of the book will die with us."

Teeleh thought about the proposal for a few seconds, then faced the eight Shataiki who stood around Billos and Darsal. "Let them go," he growled. "Today we will kill only one, not four."

TWENTY-TWO

Johnis watched as Silvie pushed Billos into her horse's saddle, then Darsal onto Johnis's horse. Silvie looked back at him, apprehension cut into her face. "Don't let him kill you, Johnis. Promise me."

What could he say to that?

"Please, just say it."

"I promise," he said. Then to Teeleh, "Give them their swords."

Another hesitation. Another nod. Two bats tossed the blades to Silvie and Billos, who dropped his. The bat hissed and shoved the sword at Darsal, who handled it well enough.

The Shataiki parted to form a path through the stadium seats, and Silvie led the way, straight up the same trail they'd arrived on.

At the top she whirled and her horse reared back, nearly dumping Billos off his back.

"Promise me, Johnis!" she cried.

"I promise!" His voice echoed through the stadium with determination. But in reality, he had no clue how to keep a promise that might also give Teeleh the book. His mind was on another promise: Teeleh had just promised to kill him, and Michal had said that when it was his time to die, he wouldn't care. But that sounded hollow in his ears. He did care, very much.

Then the two horses galloped from sight. All was quiet again except for the sounds of whispering from the thousands of Shataiki in the stands. A sea of red eyes watching, waiting. And on the platform, Johnis stood completely lost, ten feet from the huge vampire beast with draping black wings.

"Where is the book?" Teeleh finally asked.

"My deal was to tell you once they are safe in the desert. It'll take them at least half an hour."

"Why delay the inevitable?"

"When Silvie arrives safely at the desert, she'll blow her horn," Johnis said. "And if you think one of your bats can counterfeit the call, don't kid yourself. If I don't hear her horn within the hour, our deal is off."

Teeleh regarded him with his blank red eyes, standing perfectly still, like a lizard waiting for a fly to happen by. Looking at his mangy, flea-infested fur, Johnis wondered how old his carcass was. The legends had it that Teeleh had once been the most beautiful creature made by Elyon, and it had all gone to his head. Now look at him. His black skin looked like the rotting hide cut from a dead horse.

Skirmishes broke out among the bats as time slipped by. A huge battle over some disagreement in a far corner filled the stadium with such a ruckus that Johnis wondered whether the whole arena might erupt in fighting. Teeleh ignored it as if this sort of thing was to be expected among his subjects. Even welcomed.

Ten of the Shataiki ended up on the stadium floor in bloody heaps. The rest fixed their eyes back on Johnis and paid the dead bats no mind.

All the while Johnis tried to think of a way out alive. He couldn't give away the location of the book, he decided that much. As soon as Teeleh had the book in his claws, he wouldn't need Johnis. The book would keep him alive, for a while at least.

Until the disease took him.

There was always the possibility that Silvie would find a way to save him. Silvie and the book, these were his only hope of living.

Another question crossed his mind: why didn't the Roush just destroy this forest?

But the answer was found in the legends: the Roush were the subjects of men, not their masters. The Roush needed him as much as Teeleh needed him. Much more than he could imagine depended upon him, Johnis of the Middle Forest, doing the right thing at this moment.

A long, high-pitched tone floated over the stadium, and the

bats hushed. Silvie's horn. Then another long note. She'd blown the horn twice.

"They're out," Teeleh said. "Now tell me where the book is."

Johnis felt a sudden surge of desperation, which was followed immediately by sorrow. His hopes faded. Silvie hadn't doubled back to save him.

He would die alone with his secret.

"I can't tell you where the book is," he said.

"Don't try my patience!"

"You don't understand. I can't tell—"

Teeleh roared, a crackling thunderous bellow that shook the stadium and made Johnis cower. His fangs jutted down like knives from gaping, bared gums.

If Teeleh's intent had been to silence him, he'd succeeded. He'd stolen the breath of every living creature in the stadium.

The beast snapped his jaws shut with a bone-jarring crack. "Give it to me!"

"I can't."

Teeleh walked over, claws scraping on the wood planks. He leaned forward, breathing with long, noisy pulls of air. "You will," he said softly.

"I can't," Johnis said breathlessly.

The beast moved faster than Johnis could. His paw flashed up and struck him on the side of his head like a hammer. Johnis felt himself fall. Felt himself land in a heap on the wooden platform.

Then his world faded.

TWENTY-THREE

Silvie lay on her back in the darkness, not sure exactly why she was here, or, for that matter, where *here* was. It was night—or was it?

Her skin stung. Her bones ached. The disease was overtaking her body quickly.

"Darsal?"

Someone grunted nearby, and she faced the sound. Whispering and hissing filled her ears. "Let's kill her now," the snakelike voice wheezed. "He'll never know."

"Billos!" Silvie cried.

"She's awake, you coward! Make up your mind!"

She hadn't heard the voice of the smaller Shataiki until now, but she couldn't possibly mistake the similarity to Teeleh's own voice.

Silvie remembered now. She remembered all of it, from the moment they left the stadium until . . .

Until now.

SILVIE HAD LED BILLOS AND DARSAL THROUGH THE BLACK Forest while the black bats crowded, staring and whispering their treachery on all sides. But for all their snickering and bickering, the Shataiki had let them pass.

The cliffs appeared ahead without warning, and she realized that she'd missed the section where Johnis had hidden the book. But there were more than a hundred of the beasts pressing in— she couldn't double back and show them the location now!

To be honest, she wasn't sure she wanted the book anyway. It had brought them here, to this blasted black hole. Johnis was back in the stadium, giving his life for them and for the book, but no matter how hard Silvie thought about it, she couldn't think of any way to help him.

The only way to get the book, as Johnis had said, was to come back for it later. How, she didn't know.

She stopped at the edge of the Black Forest and stared at the long bridge stretching out of the bowl. The Shataiki fanned out, flying in circles, watching, always watching with those beady eyes that refused to blink.

An image of Johnis standing brave and alone on the platform with Teeleh waiting nearby filled her mind. Was she really just going to leave him? Her throat tightened, and she swallowed hard to clear it. She could never leave him. He'd given them all a chance at living by offering himself—how could she desert him?

But what choice did she have? There was no way she could take on the bats by herself. Billos and Darsal were hardly in a state to fight.

Silvie bowed her head and nudged her horse forward, allowing tears to slip down her cheeks. Elyon have mercy on them all.

They clacked up the bridge, teetering dangerously. Then they reached the top and faced the desert sands. One thing for certain, as long as the book was hidden, Teeleh would not kill Johnis. She had to attempt some kind of rescue, not only because she liked him very much, but because he was special, she realized. This boy, who had gone off into the desert because two Roush had told him to, wasn't just any ordinary boy.

Silvie grabbed the horn from her belt, faced the Black Forest below, and raised the instrument to her mouth. But before she could blow it, one of the Shataiki shrieked on her right.

She spun around in time to see its furry black body flying in, fangs bared. She had her sword in her hand, and she instinctively swung up, severing the beast's head in one smooth motion.

"Hey," Billos said. "Why'd you do that?"

Then the Shataiki descended on them, spewing hot breath and shrieks of terror. Silvie dropped the horn to the ground and spun her sword in a wide circle, scattering some of them, slicing into the flesh of others.

Darsal swung her sword as well, keeping the bats at bay. Billos cried out in protest, but she wasn't sure who he protested, them or the bats.

There were too many—she saw that almost immediately. Billos was deadweight, Darsal was slow, and Silvie couldn't hold them back on her own. Even if all three were at their best, the bats would surely overrun them.

"Run!" Silvie cried to Darsal, rolling off the horse. She slapped the stallion on the rump with the broad side of her sword. "Take Billos. Save yourselves!"

They took off without hesitation, one on each horse, galloping out to the desert. It was the only way, Silvie knew. All three of them would end up dead if they tried to take on the Shataiki in this diseased state.

The bats let Billos and Darsal go. And then they smothered Silvie. One of them must have picked up the horn and blown it, because she heard the mournful tone over the bats' shrieks. The last thing Silvie remembered was a hot mouth stretched over her face.

Until now.

"Hey!" she cried, struggling against the ropes that bound her tight. A bag was pulled off her head, and Silvie saw that it was still day. For all she knew, only minutes had passed since they'd taken her at the cliff top.

Black, angular trees rose up all around. The Shataiki that had pulled the bag up had a deep gash in its right wing, and Silvie knew her own sword had put it there.

The bat spit on her, a vile glob of yellow goo, then jerked the bag back down.

"Make it go to sleep," a Shataiki said. "Make it still."

They put her to sleep with a club.

SILVIE DREAMED OF FLYING BATS AND WHITE DESERT AND A silly Roush trying to do backflips but landing on its head instead.

A claw pinching her cheek woke her. It took her a moment to see that she was in the stadium again, with a sea of red eyes staring at her.

How . . .

"Silvie?"

Johnis's faint voice whispered her name on the right, and she tried to turn to him, only to discover that her body was bound spread-eagle to the same wheel that Billos and Darsal had been strapped to.

Beside Silvie, Johnis was tied like a spider to the web.

He was graying with the disease and bruised from more than one cuff to his face, and his eyes drooped with exhaustion. Still, he was such a handsome boy, even now. Dark hair to his shoulders and a strong jaw. Sharp nose and full lips, younger in appearance than in age. But he had the muscles of a strapping sixteen-year-old, defined by forest living.

"Johnis?" she croaked.

"Did you get it?" he asked in a barely audible whisper.

The book.

Terrible sorrow swept through her chest. "No. I'm sorry . . . They were watching."

"Billos? I heard the horn . . ."

"The bats must have blown it. Billos is free," she said. Then she started to cry because she knew what a horrible failure she was. And still this boy beside her didn't think about himself, but Billos. Billos, who'd mocked him at every turn!

Like a million insects, the Shataiki began to flitter and click their nasty tongues. Teeleh stepped into Silvie's view from behind the wheel, red eyes unchanged.

Without explaining himself, he clumped slowly over to Silvie, wings dragging behind like a tattered black wedding dress. He brought his snout close to her face and licked her cheek with his long pink tongue. The sick smell of decayed meat from his mouth made her tremble.

"Human," he breathed. "Do you love this human?"

"Get back," Johnis cried, but the sound came out in a hoarse rasp.

Teeleh ignored him and spoke to Silvie. "The kind of pain you are about to feel cannot be described," he said. "It's a pain reserved for the Horde when they die. But if you let your mind go, I think you could grow to like it."

Silvie's bones began to shake. She sagged in her ropes and begged Elyon to allow her to die.

Sobbing sounded on her right. Beside her, Johnis was crying.

His head lolled to one side, and his face was twisted in anguish, tears streaming down his cheeks. Their rock, this boy who didn't seem to know fear, was breaking.

"I'm sorry, Silvie," he whispered. Then louder, moaning with a breaking heart: "Forgive me! I'm so sorry! Please, please don't hurt her!"

Teeleh struck him in the face without looking his way.

Then his claw was on Silvie's cheek, tracing her jaw. "It's a new kind of pain," he said. "One that starts in the soul and works its way to the bones, setting them on fire. It can be done in the spine, but I prefer to do it through the neck." He drew his fingernail down past her ear.

"Stop it," Johnis whispered. "Stop it."

"Only you can stop it, boy," Teeleh said. His fingernail pressed into Silvie's skin, and she felt fire burn down her spine.

Silvie screamed.

And so did Johnis. Only his scream came with words.

"I'll tell you!" he cried. "I'll tell you. Along the path, forty-nine trees from the edge, seven trees to the left! At the base of a tree!"

Teeleh froze. Silvie's world was swimming already, but she clung to consciousness, realizing that something terrible had just happened.

The beast stepped back. Nodded. A hundred bats took flight in search of the book. And they would find it, Silvie knew.

Beside her Johnis hung his head and sobbed.

TWENTY-FOUR

J ohnis couldn't seem to stop the waves of regret and sorrow that kept washing over him. He'd failed on every level, and he'd done it in such short order. Just a few days ago he was watching the Horde football game with his father, feeling sorry for himself but safe. A nobody who made no trouble.

In four short days he'd managed to lead the three most promising new leaders of the Forest Guard into the desert where they would now die. Worse, he'd played into the hands of this beast and given him a book that contained only Elyon knew what kind of power to destroy the world.

And even worse, he'd let Silvie down. He didn't understand why, but this seemed like the greatest of his sins. Maybe because it was so personal.

"It's okay, Johnis," Silvie whispered. She'd been trying to comfort him, and even that didn't seem right to him. He should be comforting her, not the other way around.

Teeleh stood on the platform's edge, facing away from them, perhaps waiting to possess the book before killing them.

"Johnis, do you know when I told you I loved the other boy?" Silvie said.

He looked at her. What did that have to do with any of this?

"I do love him, but not more than any other boy," she said.

She paused, and he still wasn't understanding why she would discuss this while they faced their deaths.

"Do you understand what I'm trying to say?" she asked.

He studied her eyes, brimming with tears, and fought another wave of guilt. To have done this to such a beautiful, kind girl was a horrible thing.

"I think you're the kind of boy I would love," she said. "If I had known you better. You're a very good person. I want you to know that."

But he didn't feel that way at all. Still, he didn't want to discourage her by arguing at a time like this. "It's okay, Silvie. I think I love you too."

She blinked. Had he really said that? It was not what he'd meant to say, not so openly. But what difference did it make now?

Shrieking from the west signaled the Shataiki's return. They flew in a haphazard formation, two dozen of them, sweeping over the trees and into the stadium.

A particularly mangy-looking bat carried the Book of History against his chest. He settled on the platform, shot Johnis a red stare, then snaked over to Teeleh, bowed, and handed him the book.

Johnis couldn't read Teeleh's expression because his eyes were fixed and his jaw shut, but the beast's claws were trembling as he reached out for the book. He held it between his talons and traced the title, *Stories of History*, with his nail.

Not one snicker, not one cough, not one hiss or one breath could be heard from the throngs of Shataiki. Whatever was in that book was even more valuable than Johnis imagined possible.

For a long time Teeleh stared at his new treasure. Then he flung out one winged arm, eyes unmoving from the book. A tall, skinny Shataiki with drooping cheeks stepped out from behind the wheel.

Johnis hadn't noticed him flying in from the sky. Then where had he been hiding? He was taller than the others, halfway between Teeleh and the other bats, and somehow more wicked looking, if that was possible. Blue blobs of flesh hung like sacks under his eyes, and his skin was nearly bare of fur. He looked like a plucked rodent.

But it was the Book of History in his claws that sent a shiver through Johnis's bones. A second book, which he carefully handed to Teeleh. Only a single length of red twine bound this one, unlike the two bands of twine that bound the book the Roush had given Johnis.

Teeleh took the book. He now held one book in each hand,

like two counterweights. His sinewy arms quivered, and he held each delicately, as if they were eggs.

He suddenly faced the throng, lifted both books high over his head, tilted his head back, and roared at the sky. The gathering broke into earsplitting shrieks, a hundred thousand strong.

Johnis thought his eardrums might burst. He looked at Silvie, whose eyes were wide with fear.

Teeleh lowered the books and let the cries of approval wash over him. He walked to the far edge of the platform, holding the books like a mother clinging to a precious newborn child. Then he tucked them under one wing and twisted back.

"I want them to become Horde first," he snarled. "When they've both become Scabs, kill them."

Then he leaped off the platform and shot for the sky on wide leathery wings.

TWENTY-FIVE

G abil flew fast and furiously just ten feet above the western desert sand. He'd known it could all go bad, but he'd never really expected it. Not so soon, anyway. Not so terribly bad.

He'd watched from the clouds with seven other Roush and reported to Michal as soon as Johnis had offered his life for the others. But the elder Roush knew already and was preparing for the worst.

The Roush lived in the green forests, building their nests high in the canopy, where they could raise their young without fear of any human or horse stepping on them accidentally. They were blind, these humans. They couldn't see a Roush if they were punched in the nose by one. They would assume they'd hit themselves before believing a Roush from the legends, as they called history, actually existed and had just bopped them on the nose.

Lovely things, these daughters and sons of Elyon, but so pig-headed at times. Thought they knew everything. Even after chang-ing their minds five times on the same matter, they didn't pause to consider the fact that they might be wrong this sixth time as well. Heaven forbid! They would fight for the sixth opinion with as much conviction as the first!

"It's red, I say. *Red!*" one would cry.

"No, it's blue," another would respond.

"Red, you fool. Red, red, red."

"Blue for certain. Look at it from this angle and you see it's blue. Or maybe a bit green, if you think about it."

"Say what? Not green. Only an idiot would see green. More like purple, if you must. But not blue and not green."

"I say green. Definitely green. If you can't see green, you're not fit to hold a rank in the Guard."

"Purple! For the sake of Elyon, open your eyes! Any half-wit can see it's purple."

Only the arguments weren't usually about colors but some-thing more interesting, such as whether this tunic or that face marking would be appropriate to wear.

Gabil saw Billos and Darsal ahead now, slumped on the two horses, hopelessly lost. Both had grayed and lost their minds to the disease, a condition that would quickly change from the stu-pidity they currently displayed to plain deceit. The Horde could be as sharp as Teeleh's claws once their minds grew accustomed to the disease's influence, but their deception would only strengthen. He clucked with shame for them and sped up with wide sweeps of his wings.

He dove for Darsal's horse, slapping it hard on the rump with his right wing as he screamed past. The horse jumped to the right, plowing into the other horse.

"Watch it!" Billos snapped. "What are you doing?"

"It's . . . it's this blasted horse."

Gabil had to get them headed to the north, and fast. The fact that they could no longer see him in their diseased state meant he would do it the old-fashioned way, which had often proved to be disastrous in his rather extensive scope of experience. Other Roush seemed to boast of more success, but Gabil often succeeded in doing nothing more than upsetting all involved.

If they still had canteens strapped to the horses, he would have dumped the water on them to bring them out of their stupor. But the bottles had evidently been stripped off by the Shataiki.

He grabbed the reins of Billos's horse and tugged to the right. "This way, you black stallion beast!" Gabil flapped his wings hard, blowing up dust, tugging the stubborn horse.

"Hey!" Billos mumbled at no one in particular. "What are you doing? Where'd that wind come from?" His horse veered to its right, north, and Darsal's followed.

"Where're you going?" she asked dumbly.

"Where're *you* going?" he returned. "Isn't this the way?"

"Yeah, well, where are we going?"

"You don't know?"

"I thought you did."

Gabil used his claws on both of the horses' rumps this time, swiping both feet together like a double karate kick. *"Hayaa!"*

The horses bolted forward at a full gallop, with Billos and Darsal flailing and yelling. How they managed to stay on, Gabil didn't know, but he figured it served them right for not believing Johnis sooner.

He took off after the spooked horses and kept them moving with an occasional swat to the rump. "Move it, you dumb beasts! Fly, fly like the wind. *Hayaa!*"

Billos and Darsal shouted all kinds of orders at their mounts, but all were ignored. Gabil, master of the sky and now the desert, was in control.

"Hayaa!"

He kept the horses running for a full fifteen minutes before thinking that perhaps he was overdoing it. They were sweating and wheezing. What if they fell over dead from this terrified sprint of theirs? Michal had said "as quickly as possible," but Gabil wasn't completely sure how far he could push these snorting beasts.

Then an image of Johnis flashed through his mind, and he slapped the horses again. Johnis might not be able to be saved, but there was a slim chance that one or both of the books could be recovered.

They pounded over a hill, and the oasis suddenly dawned into view, a hundred yards ahead. Two fresh horses grazed by the water, ready to ride.

"Don't let them run for the water!" Billos cried. "They might drown us! Stay clear of the water!"

They were that far gone? Horde feared water. Despised it. Billos was deceived to the core.

"No, the water could be good!" Darsal said. "I think we need it."

"No! Stay clear. Only fools think water won't drown them."

"No, Billos, I need water!" She veered for the pond and, without Gabil prodding her horse from behind, managed to wrestle control back.

Billos's horse followed despite his curses. "This way, you stupid beast!" He tugged on the reins to no avail.

The horses headed straight to the water, reared to a stop, thrust their muzzles into the clear blue liquid, and began to drink. Darsal stared at the water in wonder, somewhat unsure but perhaps remembering.

Billos, on the other hand, drew his legs up and scooted to the rear of his horse, cowering. "Have you lost your mind?"

"It's blue," she said.

"It's brown! Any fool can see that."

"Blue," she said, staring.

"Brown, brown, brown, you imbecile! And what's more, it will kill you!"

Gabil flew toward the recruit, rolled into a ball at the last moment to avoid hurting him, and slammed into his back with enough force to launch the terrified Billos off his horse and into the pond with a great splash.

His cries were swallowed by the water. Darsal dropped to the sand and peered in. "Billos?"

But there was no Billos.

"Billos, are you drowning?" she cried.

Only rising bubbles answered.

Now she became truly worried. "Billos!"

He came out of the water like a rocket, gasping and grinning at once. His skin was again pink. Gabil thrust a wing at the sky and cried with delight. "Yes!"

"What are you waiting for?" Billos demanded.

Darsal smiled dumbly and fell forward like a log. The pond accepted her, then swallowed her dusty, graying body. Then she was under with Billos, who dunked himself for a second bath. Gabil paced on wobbling legs, eager to jump in himself. But he had a mission to finish. Mustn't forget the mission.

When they rose from the water moments later, Darsal threw her arms around Billos and squeezed him tight. "I could kill you!"

"For what?" he demanded, but he was laughing.

"For leaving me! Don't you ever do that again. Swear it!"

Gabil could hold himself no longer. "Hey, you two."

They whirled around, eyes like full moons. "Where did you come from?" Darsal asked.

"I've been around since the legends," he said. "Question is, where did you come from?"

Billos looked as though he'd seen a ghost. Gabil was the first Roush he'd seen. "What . . . what's that?"

"A Roush," Darsal said.

They looked at him, dripping wet, minds spinning.

"Do the words 'Black Forest' conjure up any images?" Gabil asked. "How about nasty black vampire bats with rotting breath and slimy noses? Run into any of those lately, by chance?"

"Johnis," Darsal said.

"Now you're getting the picture," Gabil said. He waddled back and forth in front of them. "It seems the sight we granted you is easily compromised. Thanks to the cleansing pool, it's back. We don't have much time, so I need you to listen to me very carefully." He wagged his finger at them. "No nonsense this time. Just trust me and listen."

They slopped out of the water, and he jumped back to avoid being splashed. Not that he minded the water, but they were still smeared with stubborn dirt and could use a proper bath.

"Now, Darsal, do you remember me showing you a karate move or two?" he said. "You'll need that when you go back in."

"Back in where?" Billos asked.

"The Black Forest, of course. The one thing these black beasts do is come at you with their teeth and claws first. So I suggest you perfect the dodge-duck-kick routine that I am best known for. I'll show—"

"We're not headed back in!" Billos cried. "We should take these catalina cacti and head back." He pointed to a group of seven large cacti on the other side of the pond. "The Horde is marching by now! Or soon. And they are coming from this side, not the other. We have to tell Thomas!"

"This book is more important than Thomas," Gabil said.

"What? How can you say that? And going back to the Black Forest would be—"

"Don't be a coward, boy. You're going back."

"Two of us against all those . . . those black beasts! It's suicide."

"Well, no one said it would be easy," Gabil snapped, feeling just a bit put off by the boy.

"Easy? We would be marching to our deaths!"

Gabil decided he'd had enough of this. They were out of time, and he hadn't yet demonstrated this move of his. "Now you listen to me, human. You were dead already. Your life isn't yours to decide any longer. You were saved by Johnis, for Elyon's love! Are you so thickheaded?"

Billos stood shivering as the water cooled on his skin.

Gabil pushed while he had the boy on his heels. "And let me tell you something else. If you hadn't been so stubborn in the beginning, none of you would be in this mess right now. Both of you should be ashamed."

"He's right!" Darsal cried, running for her horse. "We have to save Johnis and Silvie!"

Billos stood flat-footed, unsure.

Gabil hurried toward Darsal, nearly tripping over his own feet. "Wait, I haven't shown you what you'll need." He slid to a stop and threw out his wings for balance. "Watch." He ducked an imaginary punch, rolled right, and simultaneously threw his leg out in a kick.

But at the last moment he lost his balance and crashed on his rear end.

"Keep your tricks, white bat," she said. "Just tell me where the Black Forest is."

He jumped up, stunned by her audacity. "Keep my . . . ? You have almost no chance of surviving, and you still stick your nose in the air like you're the master of it? My karate could save your skinny neck, thank you very much!"

"I've seen your karate. It's cute. But—"

"I don't fight on the ground, you fool." He jumped into the air and executed the same move, ducking and rolling and kicking with perfect precision this time. *"Hayaa!"* he yelled, and dropped onto the ground, crouched for another attack.

Darsal's jaw gaped. "Wow."

"Yes, wow. They don't call me the king of the skies for nothing. Now I suggest you learn that move. As I was saying, the Shataiki attack the same way every time: fangs and claws first. Dodge those and you'll have an easy angle for their soft underbellies."

"I still don't see how we can fight off a hundred, much less ten thousand," Billos said, walking up.

"You can't," Gabil said.

"We can't? Then what's the point?"

"The point is, Johnis saved us," Darsal said. "Mount up, Billos."

"You can't defeat them," Gabil said. "But I have something

that will give you a fighting chance." He pulled out the bag he'd strung under his wing, held it out with great fanfare, and dropped it on the sand.

"What's that?"

"That," Gabil said, "is the one thing those bats fear the most."

TWENTY-SIX

Qurong, leader of the Horde, sat on his stallion and gazed eastward. It would take them nearly a day to move the large army to the canyons along the forest's edge. It would be another half day through the canyons and into the forest, provided the Guard hadn't been alerted. The cliffs gave their enemy a natural barrier that made his task difficult.

But the last report had sounded an all-clear. Thomas's Guard was still camped on the east, where a smaller Horde force made daily raids to keep them busy.

Still no sign of the missing recruits. Dead, the word was. Killed by the desert. Even the priest had proclaimed it, though with some coercion from Qurong. He would kill that snake of a priest yet. All his talk of Teeleh and these blasted missing books was enough to drive him mad, especially in the wake of losing the boy from his own custody.

He looked back at the horses, more than a hundred thousand of them, all mounted and awaiting his command. And behind, three hundred thousand foot soldiers, armed to the necks with sickles and hammers and spears, as well as a sword for each.

"We're ready?" he asked the traitor, who sat astride a horse beside him.

The man looked eastward for a long time, making Qurong wonder if he'd ever consider going back to the forests. He was fully Horde, but then again, so were their spies, who bathed and became Forest Dwellers for the cause. Even so, what could this man tell Thomas that he didn't already know? The Forest Guard already knew all too well how to kill Horde.

"As ready as we will ever be," the traitor finally said.

Qurong lifted his hand, then lowered it slowly. The massive army began to move, a sea of gray flesh, horse meat, and enough metal to sever the head of every living creature in the forests.

"So it begins," Qurong said.

"So it begins," the traitor breathed.

"LET ME GIVE YOU MY NAME," THE TALLER SHATAIKI SAID, plodding slowly across the platform in front of Johnis, arms clasped behind his back. "My name is Alucard. Let me tell you what it means. Demon. Do you know what a demon is?"

Johnis hardly heard him. His mind was fogged by the disease, though he desperately tried to hold on to reason. He managed to think about the book that Teeleh had taken such delight in. He didn't know why the beast had trembled with joy when he'd taken possession of the second book, but it couldn't mean anything good for humans.

Several delirious hours had passed, and the sun blazed bright and hot overhead. Except for a few Shataiki that flapped about the bleachers, the amphitheater had emptied when Teeleh had soared skyward. Four of the Shataiki stood guard on the stage with this demon wretch, waiting for Johnis and Silvie to finish their transformation into Scabs.

Beside him, Silvie was crying again. But in his own foggy thinking he was having difficulty determining *why* he should comfort her, much less *how* he could comfort her. He began to think that she sounded a bit like a bat.

"You don't even know why the books are so powerful, do you?" something said. Oh yes—Alucard, the Shataiki bat, was speaking again. "I could torture you with needles, but the full knowledge of your failure will cause more pain."

"What's that smell?" Johnis heard himself mumble.

The bat stopped pacing. "I would think that's your flesh rotting," he said.

But it is more, Johnis thought. *Something smells vaguely familiar.*

"The books have the full creative power of will," the Shataiki said. "They can influence the power of human decisions. They can make the word become flesh. They can make a moon red with blood or a soul black with lies."

"'Destroy the world,'" Johnis whispered, remembering the inscription on the rock. *In the west, the Dark One seeks Seven to destroy the world.*

"Yes. Something like that. The seven original books are the keys to heaven and hell. Teeleh is the rightful prince of both. He holds two in his library below." The Shataiki gave a hissing cackle. "So close, yet so very far."

"Smoke," Johnis breathed, barely aware of his own voice.

"The smoke of hell is what you'll soon be . . ."

The bat stopped midsentence. As a matter of fact, Johnis *did* smell smoke. The old bat was smoldering like a trampled fire, perhaps. Dust to dust, fire to fire, ash to ash.

A chorus of high-pitched shrieks carried across the hot wind from the east. Probably just more Shataiki squawking over a piece of rotten fruit or a rat they'd found.

Alucard whirled around and faced eastward.

Johnis lifted his eyes to clouds that boiled on the horizon. *Odd,* he thought. *Those clouds weren't there a few minutes ago. Is rain coming? It never rains in the desert, but what about here?*

He didn't want it to rain. Rain would mean water, and water was a dreadful thing. Wasn't it? Water would kill you if you let it. Drown you. Which was why he'd rather walk through the fires of hell than drown in a lake.

"Fire!" one of the guarding bats cried. "It's fire!"

Alucard seemed to have frozen into a tree. But his trance didn't last long. His wings snapped wide like a black kite, and he leaped off the platform with surprising strength. "Fire!" he screeched.

Fire?

"ENOUGH!" DARSAL YELLED ABOVE THE HUGE CRACKLING flames that licked at the black trees. "We're out of time!"

Billos was standing in his stirrups, swinging his sword in wide circles with both hands as if it were a club. No fewer than ten Shataiki came at him from all sides, screaming in death-defying dives.

His blade connected with the lead bat, cutting its cry off at the neck. He dodged another, knocking it wide with his forearm, then drove down on the beast's back.

His horse trampled the bat and reared. Billos was now in his element, showing why he'd been selected by Thomas as one of the four greatest fighters to join the Forest Guard.

Darsal threw her flaming torch into a pile of dried moss and snatched her sword up just in time to defend against the jaws of another bat who, seeing her let loose of her fire, dove in expecting an easy prey. Not so. Darsal was nearly as efficient with her blade as Billos was. She ducked in the way Gabil had suggested and thrust the blade up through the bat's jaw, pinning its mouth shut. Then she flung it behind her and screamed at another bat soaring in.

This Shataiki thought better of it and broke off its attack just short of her blade's reach.

The black bats were terrified of fire—this alone had given Darsal and Billos the advantage. Gabil had sworn nothing less when he'd given them the resin and flint.

"Set the forest on fire!" he'd said. "As long as you're near fire, the bats will hesitate. Burn the whole forest and ride the edge of the flames all the way to Teeleh's lair."

"How do we get out?"

"That's Michal's part," the Roush had said. "Go. Hurry! And don't forget about the karate!"

They'd lit the torches before reaching the cliff's edge, then approached at a full gallop, with such speed that the few Shataiki on the bowl's lip had been thrown into confusion. By the time the bats realized what was happening, Darsal and Billos had their horses running down the unsteady bridge and were warding off the bats with fire.

At the edge of the black trees, they had taken off in opposite directions, as planned. Billos went north, Darsal south, thrusting fire into the foliage as they galloped.

As Gabil had promised, the undergrowth and the black trees rising from it went up like a tinderbox. It was almost as if they were soaked in resin, begging to be burned.

Fires of hell.

They'd gone a mile in each direction, then doubled back and met at the path that led into the forest.

Already huge flames rose to the height of the tallest trees, blasting Darsal with heat. Only the bravest Shataiki endured the smoke now, again as Gabil had promised. The winds carried the fire toward them. Toward the center of the forest. Toward the stadium.

Toward Johnis and Silvie.

"Hurry!" Darsal cried.

Billos screamed at three fleeing bats. At the moment she could not think of a man she would rather have by her side than Billos. He was better with a sword than most of the seasoned fighters who defended the forests.

"Go, go!"

They went at a full gallop. The fire behind them was making its own wind now, crackling like thunderclaps as the black trees exploded with heat. What if it was too big? What if they couldn't outrun the flames?

Darsal glanced back and saw that the flames were leaping high above the trees, licking at the sky hungrily. Heat rode their backsides, pushing the horses faster. Even the bravest Shataiki had now fled the fire.

"We're going too slow!" Billos cried, echoing her concern.

They pounded through the Black Forest, twisting and turning with the trail. Here nothing was straight, not even a path that could have easily been laid down in an orderly fashion, right through the trees. But the Shataiki obviously didn't know the meaning of straight.

The flames roared to the rear, gaining, now only fifty yards back.

Darsal cursed the crooked path and drove harder, slapping her horse's rump with the broad side of her sword. "Faster!"

The stallion needed no encouragement, and she gave it up, holding tight to the reins in one hand and her sword in the other.

"Which way?" Billos screamed from behind as they approached the split in the trail.

Darsal veered right. "Hurry!"

The fire was gaining. Her hair might go up in flames at any moment.

Billos pulled up beside her, though there was hardly enough room for two horses abreast on this trail. She saw why—his horse's tail was singed! Billos was hunkered down, trying to keep the heat from burning his neck. She let him surge ahead.

The stadium suddenly opened up before them, a huge oblong hole in the ground. Now they had two options: they could slow and risk being burned from behind, or they could plunge into the bleachers and risk a bad fall.

Billos chose the latter, urging his horse even faster. He launched the stallion over the lip, trusting the mount to find its own footing. It sailed into the air, over the stepped risers, dropped ten feet, and crashed into the stone steps just ahead of Darsal's own horse, which launched itself into the air just behind.

This was why picking the horses was such an honor for the best fighters. Both steeds landed at a full run and descended into the stadium without slowing, sure-footedly placing their hooves in precisely the right spot.

The fire reached the edge of the stadium above them and shot out with searing orange heat. But without more fuel the flames collapsed back on themselves and swept to the right and left, ringing the stadium.

Billos and Darsal reached the field and raced across the flat ground toward the platform where Johnis and Silvie slumped in their ropes. They looked to be unconscious on the great wheel. Grayed with disease and lost to the world.

"The water, quickly," Darsal yelled, searching the perimeter for signs of Shataiki. There were none that she could see. For the moment.

They slid from their horses, pulled out the bags of blue water they had filled at the pond, and bounded onto the platform.

"Just dump it?" Billos asked.

Without answering, Darsal yanked out the cork, lifted the leather bag over Johnis's head, and began to splash the water over his face and shoulders. It ran down his chest like a river.

The transformation wasn't unlike watching cool water wash over parched, dusty skin, or rain falling upon a dried riverbed. Each flake of flesh touched was restored to fresh skin on contact.

Johnis jerked his head up and gasped, just as Billos dumped his water over Silvie. Darsal continued to pour, eager for every square inch of Johnis's body to be rid of the disease. More water, over his head now, flooding his eyes and nose with the healing water.

Johnis sputtered and coughed, and Darsal drained the last of it over him.

"My face," he said. "Wipe my face!"

He was practically drowning in the water, she realized. Beside them, Silvie began to sputter as well. Billos was showing no more restraint.

Darsal reached up and wiped the water from his face. Johnis blinked the last of the moisture away.

"Darsal?"

"Who did you expect? Teeleh?" She gave him a grin.

His eyes scanned the fire sweeping on each side. He locked his gaze back on her. "You came back . . ."

"Forgive me."

"You . . ." Johnis seemed too surprised to think clearly. "You came back."

"I was a fool to leave you. I'm so sorry."

"But you came back!" he cried.

"You can kiss her later," Silvie said sharply. "For the sake of Elyon, get us off of here!"

"You were right, Scrapper," Billos said. "I owe you an—"

"Cut us down!" Silvie cried.

"The fire won't keep them away for long," Darsal said, yanking out her knife. "We have to get out of here."

"Not until we have the books," Johnis said.

"That's ridiculous," Billos snapped. "We're in the middle of the Black Forest, if you hadn't noticed."

"We came for the books," Johnis said.

Billos wouldn't let go. "The Shataiki will be swarming—"

"Enough, Billos!" Johnis shouted. "I will not leave without the Books of History!"

That shut the boy down as if he'd been forced to swallow a cork.

"Books, as in more than one?" Darsal asked.

"Books. He has two. We can't leave without them."

"And do you have any clue where these books are?"

Johnis took a deep breath and swallowed. "Yes, I think I do."

TWENTY-SEVEN

re you sure it's a fire?" Thomas demanded, marching with Mikil down the main path toward the barracks. "In the west, you say?"

"Have you ever seen a black cloud rise from the earth?" Mikil said. "It's a fire, and it's farther out than we've ever ventured."

"Horde, then," Thomas said.

"Maybe."

"To the west, not the east."

"The question is, how many?" Mikil said. "First our four recruits go missing in the west, and now we see a large fire on the western horizon. I don't like it."

Thomas frowned. "Neither do I." He looked to the east, where the main body of their forces was entrenched. "We've had no significant Horde activity except for these persistent raids on the east for three days now."

"No."

"Then maybe the camp on the east is a ruse," Thomas said. "They could be attacking from the west. Is that possible?"

Her eyes were wide, and sweat beaded her forehead. "It could be. But if we move our forces from our defensive positions in the east, we'll leave that flank exposed."

"We have the high ground on the west because of the cliffs. How many fighters could hold the cliffs? Five thousand?"

"Ten," Mikil said. "At the very least."

Thomas closed his eyes and tried to settle his frayed nerves. It was like this often now, flirting with death at every turn.

"Take half our forces, five thousand. And the thousand new recruits. Stand them on the cliffs. Make them look like ten. Do whatever you have to—just show force. If they are planning on a surprise, even a smaller force will throw them. Then send a scouting party one day out into the western desert. We hold the other five thousand in their positions in the east for now, but have them ready to move if word comes that we've been tricked."

"Yes, sir," Mikil said. "You'll stay here in the village?"

"Yes, until I know for sure. No more word on the recruits?"

"None. They're lost, Thomas. I'm sorry, but there's no way they could have survived this long in the desert."

"I don't know. I'm still not convinced."

"Then let me go," Mikil said.

"Out into the desert?"

"I'll lead the scouting party. For you, sir."

He thought about her suggestion, then nodded. "Take ten of our best—and extra water. Head directly toward this smoke. One day out, no more. Let's see what secrets the desert is hiding from us."

IT WAS MORE OF A HUNCH THAN SPECIFIC KNOWLEDGE, BUT Alucard's statement that Teeleh's lair was below and not very far had gnawed at Johnis's subconscious from the moment he'd heard it. He couldn't shake the suspicion that there was more to this stadium than met the eye.

He dropped to the ground and ran behind the platform.

Actually, the single greatest tip-off had been Alucard's sudden appearance with Teeleh's Book of History. He'd come from the back, Johnis remembered. And he hadn't seen the beast fly in.

Rough-hewn planks formed a wall around the platform, like a skirt that hid whatever lay below. Johnis ran the perimeter and pulled up hard at the very back.

There, almost exactly as he'd pictured it in his mind's eye, was a gate made from the same planks. He pulled it open and peered in. Stairs cut from wet, mossy stone descended into the ground. The putrid smell of death that rose around him made him blanch involuntarily.

This was it! He knew to the core of his bones. The Dark One's lair awaited below.

Johnis returned to the front. "Wait here. Watch the horses. And if you have any trouble, blow the horn."

"Where are you going?" Silvie demanded. "I'm going with you!"

"No, you're not. Teeleh's either down there or he's out because of the fire. If he's still in the lair, it's finished; you have to accept that. Not one of us stands a chance against that beast. No use in all of us risking our necks."

"I was under the impression that we were already doing that," Billos said.

They ignored him. Darsal threw Johnis an unlit torch. "Take this with you. One strike and it will burn."

Johnis looked at it. This was what they must've started the fire with. Who'd given it to them was anyone's guess, but an image of a fuzzy white Roush came to his mind.

The moist, mossy stone steps leading down were best gripped with claws, not boots. They twisted to the left, forming a circular staircase, darker with each step down. He lit the torch and stared downward. Yellow light touched the rock walls, but even this seemed to be absorbed by the blankness below.

Johnis forced his way down twenty, maybe even thirty, steps, then stepped off the last worn stone into a circular atrium. Same dark mossy walls; same putrid, sulfuric odor. The floor had been worn smooth by countless padding feet. The ceiling was low, and the black smoke from his torch fanned out directly over his head.

Straight ahead of him the curving wall was broken by a large, glistening black door with a corroded handle. Staring at that tarred door was like staring into the heart of Teeleh. Johnis suddenly hoped it was locked so that he could turn and run.

He stood shivering, knowing that time was too short. Billos was right—the Shataiki might be fleeing the fire, but with so many of them in the forest, they would be swarming back soon enough.

He stepped up to the black door, reached for the rusty handle, and hesitated. He watched his trembling fingers for a long ten seconds, then touched it.

He'd half expected a flash of darkness. Another vision of the dark man-beast reaching for his throat. But nothing happened. The handle was cold.

He turned the latch and pushed the door gently. It opened with a soft squeal of metal. A puff of warm, musty air brushed his face and blew the flame, which wavered and crackled. His heart thumped in his ears, but he detected no sign of Teeleh.

Then he stepped in. Into Teeleh's lair that had surely been carved from the pit of the earth hundreds, maybe thousands, of years ago.

He faced six smaller, arched doors set in stone, forming a twenty-foot semicircle. Water dripped somewhere deep behind these walls. The doors presented him with another decision, and at the moment he was hating decisions, particularly ones that all seemed to lead deeper into trouble.

But time was going. Maybe already gone.

He quickly tried the door on his right.

Locked. Thank Elyon.

The next door, also locked. And the next, and the next, and the next.

Thank Elyon. He didn't want to be down here any longer.

Johnis grabbed the last handle and pushed, expecting to be given the liberty of fleeing back through the main door, up the circular stairwell, and out into fresher air to announce that Billos was right. All was lost; they would have to go back.

But the door swung in silently. He jumped back, startled.

Now he had no choice. He had to go in. And so he did, just two steps.

The door opened to a tunnel carved out of stone, tall enough for a man to walk easily. Or a beast. The walls glistened with a moist gel or resin. Standing so close to them, Johnis was sure the terrible rotten odor that plugged his nostrils came from this gel.

Here and there his torchlight showed huge pink roots that ran along the slimy walls. The cobblestoned tunnel floor ran wet into the earth. The passageway was terrifying in itself, but still no sign of the Shataiki bat.

Johnis started to walk down the tunnel, holding the crackling torch in front of him.

Farther into the earth. Farther from his comrades. The tunnel seemed to stretch into darkness forever. He stopped and considered returning. Thinking with his heart was one thing; madness was another.

And this was the latter.

He stared at one of the pink roots to his right. It was a good six inches in diameter, moist and smooth except for round rings every few inches. Like a huge earthworm.

The root suddenly bunched up slightly and slid forward. Johnis's heart skipped a beat. Two beats.

It *was* a worm. And the worm was sliding forward through the thin layer of worm gel coating the wall.

Panicked, he tore his feet from the ground and bolted forward, deeper, screaming to himself that he was going the wrong direction.

He should be going back! That's what his mind cried. *Back, back, back, you fool!*

But he wasn't thinking with his mind. He knew that he couldn't go back, so he ran on. The worms lined the tunnel walls, leaving long trails of slime in their wake.

For a brief moment he wondered what that stuff would taste like, because although it made no sense to him, he did feel an odd attraction to it.

You're in Teeleh's lair, Johnis. This must be where the disease was first born. This is where the worms feed on the souls of humans and leave sludge behind. You have no business being in this place.

A room suddenly gaped on his right, and he slid to a stop. Beyond a large wrought-iron gate sat a wooden desk, and in front of the desk, an old stone stool. Three candlesticks stood on the desk, along with an inkwell, closed at the moment. Bookcases lined the walls, filled with dozens of dusty, leather-bound volumes.

Teeleh's library? Or lair? Perhaps both.

The vision he'd seen in the desert, when the man had told him it was all about the library—"The Horde is in the library," he'd said, or something similar—came to mind. It was all connected. Books, visions, power, lairs, libraries, killers, Horde.

Teeleh.

The dark man-beast he'd seen when touching the book with his blood. *But more than Teeleh,* he thought. It still didn't all add up.

Johnis reached for the latch, found it unlocked, and pulled the gate open, wincing at the loud screeching of metal against metal. He glanced both ways down the tunnel and heard no sounds of pursuit, only the continued dripping of water on stone. *Drip, drip, drip.*

He walked in slowly, trying not to breathe too loudly. Looking around the room, he couldn't help thinking he'd been here before, in this very room.

Several volumes sat on a table at the center. Their titles had been rubbed away. A green book, a black book, and a red book. In contrast, the books on the shelves were shades of dark brown and bound in leather.

Words had been drawn on one wall. Strange scribblings that meant nothing to him:

Welcome to Paradise.

Born of Black and White

Eaten with worms

I'm a Saint. a Sinner. a Siren of the word

[Some words had been smudged here.]

Showdown at midnight.

Born of Black and White. Could that mean writing? Or Teeleh? Or a skunk, for all he knew.

Eaten with worms. Surely the worms in the tunnel.

Saint, Sinner, Siren. Only Elyon knew. As with the last line, *Showdown at midnight.* A coming confrontation of epic proportions, waged at night.

Johnis turned his eyes to the desk. He'd almost missed them because there was a dirty rag draped over them, but there in the light of his torch he saw the edges of two books bound in red twine.

Two Books of History. The black one from Michal, and a dark brown one.

For a moment Johnis couldn't move. Then he couldn't stop moving.

He dashed to the desk, snatched up both books, whirled around, and ran from the room, mind fixed on one thing and one thing only.

Out. He had to get out.

Still no sign of Teeleh.

He raced back down the tunnel, slipping twice and very nearly sprawling on his backside. The door to this tunnel was still open, and he flew through, gripping the corner of the wall as he exited. His fingers sank into the gel that coated the stone, and for one crazy moment he thought about sucking the gel from his hand. The tunnels were making him mad.

Flinging the stuff off with a snap of his wrist, he bounded out of the atrium, up the steps, and into the open air, letting the gate smack shut behind him.

He'd made it. He stood in a crouch for several quick breaths, grappling with the accomplishment. Then he stifled a whoop of victory and raced around the platform.

"I have them!" he cried, unable to contain himself any longer. "I have them both!"

No response. Did they hear him?

"I have them! Silvie, I have both of them." He rounded the corner and saw Silvie, Darsal, and Billos by the horses, backs to him.

"I have . . ."

He pulled up hard when he saw what they were looking at. The sky was still filled with smoke, a good thing.

But now the bleachers were filled with Shataiki, who'd come either to escape the fire or to butcher the thieves who would take their books.

A bad thing.

For a while Johnis just stared, refusing to accept the meaning of this sudden turn of events. They were trapped. There was no way out from here, was there?

He set his jaw and strode past the others, suddenly furious at how it was all ending. He'd believed the Roush and crossed the desert and risked his life and found Teeleh's lair. All for this?

Johnis faced the black beasts, thrust both books into the air as Teeleh had done, and screamed at the sky.

"I have them!"

The words filled him with courage.

"These books belong to Elyon, not to Teeleh! I have them. Go ahead, you filthy beasts, try to take them. Step forward and see what Elyon makes of his books."

As one, the Shataiki crept forward onto the field, like a thick carpet of oil. They pressed toward the platform, one step, then two, then on, plodding slowly, silent and deliberate.

"Now you've done it, Scrapper," Billos said softly.

Johnis walked calmly to his horse, stuffed both books into the saddlebag, and withdrew his sword. He'd yet to swing it, he realized. Now was as good a time as any to baptize the blade with blood.

Shataiki blood.

He raised it and pointed at the bats who were still approaching like a slow-moving tide.

"For Elyon, you filthy beasts. When you take up against us, you take up against Elyon!"

First Silvie, then Billos and Darsal, stepped up beside him, blades by their sides.

"This is it," Darsal said.

"Yes, this is it." Silvie breathed out. "This is definitely it."

Billos swished his sword once. "Duck, dodge, kick."

"Karate," Darsal said. "Watch their fangs and claws. Go for their soft underbellies."

Silvie nodded. "You do realize there are too many. Way too many."

"Yes, too many," Darsal agreed.

"They'll kill us," Silvie said.

"Yes, they will," Billos said.

The black throng stopped no more than thirty paces off, red eyes glowing, waiting for what, Johnis didn't know.

"The books are mine," a gravelly voice growled from high on their right. Johnis saw Teeleh for the first time, perched on the stadium's lip. "Rip them limb from limb!"

The Shataiki threw themselves forward with a chorus of shrieks. Johnis braced himself, ready to cut through.

As if drawn by the onrushing Shataiki, white smoke began to pour over the eastern lip of the stadium, where black trees had stood tall just an hour ago. It spilled in silently, a blanket of fluff, coursing over the rings of seats carved from stone, flying low and fast and boiling with power.

Johnis caught his breath and nearly forgot about the front line of rushing black bats—because this wasn't white smoke flooding the stadium.

This was white Roush.

Thousands of them, so thick you could swear they were a flood of cotton balls, so silent you'd guess a drifting cloud.

And at the head of them were two he recognized immediately: Michal and Gabil.

"Roush!" Johnis screamed.

That one word pierced the din and reached the ears of the mangy black bats, only because they all were listening warily for it.

The Shataiki spun their thin necks as one, saw the wall of white, and took off straight up, streaking for the sky.

Johnis did manage to take one swing, and he felt his sword strike flesh. A black rag of a bat plopped dead on the field in front of him.

Then the sky was dark with Roush and Shataiki locked in ferocious battle. They tore into each other, and from what Johnis could see, the Roush didn't have the advantage. Perhaps a little, but not in the way he expected.

"This way!" a thin voice cried. Johnis spun and saw Gabil pulling two horses forward. "Hurry, you must take the books out!"

Johnis and Silvie threw themselves on one of the horses. Darsal and Billos climbed onto the other.

"Out, out!"

"What about you? You have to come!"

"I have some karate to deliver, boy!" A dead Roush slammed into the platform to their left. Gabil looked at his fallen comrade, made a terrible face Johnis didn't know he was capable of, and whirled back.

"Stop at the pool," Gabil cried, leaping into the air. "Then back to the forests on the horses you find there! Do not stop until you are safe!"

Johnis glanced up to his right and saw that Teeleh was gone. A Shataiki and a Roush locked in each other's claws hurled past them, smashed into the ground, and rolled to a stop. Neither got up.

How many would die for them today?

"Let's go!" Darsal cried. She bolted up the stadium seats, with Johnis close behind.

The forest was burned to a crisp and still smoldered hot. The horses ran at a gallop, over fallen logs and smoking branches. It wasn't an easy ride, but the path to the desert was free of Shataiki.

The Shataiki were behind them, killing the Roush.

TWENTY-EIGHT

Qurong paced on the sand in front of his horse, feeling heat rise from the blasted desert, but more so from his own skin.

"Well?" he snapped.

The traitor tossed him the eyeglass he'd introduced to the Horde just months earlier. A device for farseeing that Thomas Hunter had come up with.

Qurong caught the gourd, lifted it to one eye, and peered at the distant cliffs. The line of Forest Guard started as far north as he could see and stretched south, past the device's limits.

"It's the smoke," the priest hissed behind him. "Didn't I tell you there was black magic in the air?"

"Smoke is not magic, you fool,"

"This smoke is. There *is* no forest behind us!"

"What lies *ahead* of us is the issue now," the traitor said. "We can deal with this fire soon enough. But looking ahead I see a slaughter."

Qurong flung the glass at him. "*Their* slaughter, you mean. I won't let this string of fighters perched like proud cockatoos foil my plan! We go in!" He swung onto his horse. He'd become so accustomed to the pain of sudden movement that he gave it no mind.

"Then you'll lose your army," the traitor said. "You can't keep going back—"

"Don't talk to me of our old ways!" Qurong roared.

"Then be my guest. Commit your men to their deaths."

Qurong breathed heavily through his nose. There would come a day when he'd leave the fighting to his generals. Perhaps to the traitor himself. But today he commanded.

"You can see it, can't you?" the traitor asked softly. "They have the upper hand. Their archers will kill most of our horses in the canyons from their positions above. Like fish in a barrel."

"Fish in a barrel?"

The traitor hesitated. "A saying Thomas uses. The point is, this plan has been compromised. We'd be better off attacking from the east, where there are no cliffs."

"But our forces are here! Because of you, I will add."

"Better to fight another day," the traitor said.

And Qurong knew he was right.

"We've been foiled by black magic," the priest of Teeleh said behind them.

"Curse your black magic!" Qurong snapped.

The priest didn't flinch. There was something to this whole mess, this business of Teeleh and missing books, that Qurong thought might end up playing into his hands.

"Your decision?" the traitor asked.

"We fight another day," Qurong said and spit to one side.

The traitor dipped his head. "Wise. And that day will be sooner than you think."

Then he did something that Qurong found very strange indeed. He withdrew a silver ring from his pocket, rode to a boulder jutting from the sand—the only such rock for a thousand paces—and placed the ring on top.

"What's the meaning of this?" Qurong demanded.

"Do you want your battle?"

"I don't see what a ring has to do with battle."

"But I do." He took out his knife, cut his finger, and soaked a small piece of cloth with the blood. Then he placed the cloth under the ring.

"Enough with your secrets," Qurong said.

The priest spoke confidently. "It's the language of black magic!"

The traitor returned to their sides. "No. But it's a language that is as strong. They will know. Believe me, they will know."

TWENTY-NINE

ather! Father!" screamed Thomas's daughter, Marie, running like the wind through the front door. "They've been found!"

Thomas bolted up from the table, spilling his beetroot soup. He snatched his sword from the wall and took a step toward her before he'd had time to process her claim.

Waiting here in the village while his officers tried to determine where the battle would come from had driven sleep from him for the past two days. Now his daughter was informing him that the Horde had been found. He had to get to his men!

But this was Marie crying at him. Why would his young daughter bring news of the Horde?

"The Horde?" he demanded. "Who? What're you talking about?"

"Johnis! Billos, Silvie, Darsal! Your recruits are back!"

Thomas closed his eyes, stilled the tremor in his tired limbs, and stepped back to his chair. "Don't be silly, child." He sat again, surveying the mess he'd made. The children had turned the four dead recruits into heroes and played games around the clock, pretending to be them. Now they actually believed their games. It was going too far.

"This is nothing to play with!"

His son, Samuel, sprinted in, face white as a pastry puff. "Father, they're entering the stadium now!"

Rachelle stood from the end of the table. "Thomas?" Her voice made it clear that she saw truth here. At the very least, Marie and Samuel believed their story to be true.

Could it be?

"They're in the stadium now? With Mikil?"

"All four," Samuel said, "with Mikil and another ten of the Guard. The village is coming out to see them." He whirled and was gone in a blur of arms and legs, followed by Marie.

"I told you!" Marie cried. "I told you!"

Thomas tore from the house, vaulted one of the rosebushes at the end of his walk, and ran toward the wide path that split the circular village like a spoke of a wheel.

He heard them before he found them, only because at least a thousand others had already found them and were ushering them into the stadium. Dusk was falling; the daily Gathering would begin soon. If Marie and Samuel were right about the recruits, these four would be the talk of the forest for a week.

He ran past a few hundred villagers hurrying to the amphitheater, spun into the passage that led to the field, and ran toward the cries and whistles of approval.

He could see them now. A group of roughly fifteen Forest Guard led by Mikil had stopped in the middle, facing the field entrance in expectation of his arrival. This was Mikil's idea, no doubt. She was making a spectacle of this turn of events, knowing it would bring courage to them all.

The stadium was filling as word spread. Thomas slowed to a walk and stepped onto the field. Almost immediately the crowd saw him and hushed.

Four stallions were in the center of the group, and on these horses sat Johnis, Billos, Darsal, and Silvie. But he saw something else now. Two long poles were strapped to their saddles, making a stretcher.

Only this stretcher didn't carry the wounded. It carried four large catalina cacti.

Thomas hid his smile and stopped twenty paces from them. For a long moment no one moved. What he saw next struck a chord of pride in his heart.

Johnis, the youngest of the four, dismounted, walked up to him, and knelt on one knee. "Your cacti, sir. Forgive our tardiness."

So, whatever had happened, Johnis had emerged as the leader. The other three were on the ground now, kneeling.

"Stand up." Thomas waved them to their feet. "Stand up and be counted."

They stood.

"You're alive," Thomas said.

No response.

"How did it happen?"

Johnis hesitated. "We got lost and were taken captive," he said. "A large Horde army marched in from the west but turned back when they saw the Guard on the cliffs. We were afraid you'd been fooled by their forces on the east, sir."

Thomas glanced at Mikil, who nodded. "Four hundred thousand strong, by our estimates. They were turned back."

So it was true! Qurong was becoming wiser in his ways of war. A year ago he never would have thought to try such trickery. The Horde was learning fast, much too fast.

"And the smoke we saw?" Thomas asked.

Again Johnis hesitated as if unsure how to answer. "There was a fire?" he asked. "Then I would assume it came from the Horde or their allies, the Shataiki."

"Shataiki?"

"Figure of speech, sir."

Billos and Darsal had been beaten and cut, he saw. Johnis and Silvie had bruises, but not like their comrades. All of them wore tattered tunics, stripped of armor. The poor souls had endured far more than he could guess. But they were alive, and at the moment he took more pride in these four than in any other members of the Forest Guard.

Regardless of what Johnis said, Thomas knew the smoke that

had warned them had more to do with these four than they let on. There was too much coincidence to assume otherwise.

The crowd continued to swell, staring, eagerly listening for what Thomas, their supreme commander, would say to these four.

"Send word to the army," Thomas said to Mikil. "Hold on both fronts, and let the Horde know that we aren't fooled. I'll join you in the morning."

"Yes, sir." She kicked her horse and galloped past him, headed for the barracks.

Thomas paced before them. "Your time to bring the cacti back has passed," he said.

Johnis bowed. "And you would be remiss to instate us in the Forest Guard after such a dismal failure."

Thomas could not hold back a small grin. "Is that so?"

"I think so, sir."

"On the other hand, you have done what no other Forest Guard could do by warning us of the Horde in the west. We would have faced wholesale slaughter if you had brought the catalina cacti back on time."

None of them spoke.

"How about you, Darsal? What say you?"

"I say I would give my life for the Guard. But the choice is yours."

"I see. And you, Silvie?"

"I say that Johnis should not only serve in the army, but command an army. The rest of us, I'm not so sure of."

"Really? And why should Johnis command an army? He's only sixteen."

"Because he thinks with his heart."

There was more to this story. Thomas would get to the bottom of it sooner or later. But none of that mattered at the moment. Johnis had the circle mark on his neck. That alone qualified him.

"And you, Billos?"

"We killed our first Horde, sir. And we escaped their clutches. I think that should qualify us for service, if nothing more."

"Johnis!" someone cried behind Thomas. He turned and saw that his father, Ramos, stood in the same entrance Thomas had used, panting from a long run. His face beamed, wet with sweat. "You're . . ." He stumbled forward, spreading his arms. "You're alive!"

A slight smile crossed Johnis's face.

Ramos turned in a circle, screaming out to those gathered now. "My son is found! My son! What did I tell you?"

He'd "told" the crowd nothing, of course. This comment was directed at Thomas.

He rushed up to Johnis, collided with him roughly, lifted him in a great bear hug, and spun him around. "My son is home!"

Then he kissed his son on one cheek, then the other, and ended on his nose—a great bearded rub that no one in any other circumstance could possibly appreciate.

Poor Johnis hung like a straw doll. But he was grinning when his father plopped him back down and ruffled his hair.

"I knew it!"

Thomas faced the crowd. He knew what they wanted. It was the same thing he wanted.

He lifted both arms. "I say this day that Johnis, Billos, Silvie, and Darsal have proven their worth!" he cried. "I say they have fulfilled the mission and can serve by my side as squad leaders. And I say that on this day, each shall be given the rank of sergeant."

The stadium erupted in a roar of approval.

"Welcome home your Guard!" Thomas thundered. "Give them your blessing. Tonight the celebration is for them!"

The dancing began then, in the stands, as thousands shouted with fists raised in salute.

Johnis stared around, dumbstruck. Thomas took his jaw and turned his head. The mark was still there. "Blessing, lad. Don't resist your calling. And let's keep it to ourselves, shall we?"

The boy simply stared at him with wide eyes.

Someday Johnis will be a king, Thomas thought.

A king who listens to his heart.

THIRTY

The night went long, and the celebration was far more than Johnis could handle. The line of proud well-wishers who came by to shake their hands and speak words of encouragement seemed to never end.

And he was pulled into more than a few dances with young women who suddenly thought he was the moon itself. Billos ate it all up. Even Darsal took it all in stride. But Johnis and Silvie were the quiet ones, and the attention was overwhelming for them.

Still, he was rather proud, he supposed. They had done good, never mind that they'd stumbled into it all.

The celebration had finally wound down and the fires had been put out. Soon dawn would gray the eastern sky. But there was still business to be done. As agreed, the four stole away and met in one of the gazebos by the lake to get their story straight.

"Well, what do you think of that?" Billos beamed. "We're heroes, by the stars."

"This will only make things more difficult," Johnis said.

"Have you lost your mind, Scrapper?" Billos snorted. Then he clapped him on the back. "You know I don't mean that in a bad way."

"What?"

"Scrapper. It's just an endearing term that will help keep you humble. Though Elyon knows you deserve more respect than any one of us."

"Then don't call him Scrapper," Silvie said.

"It's okay," Johnis said. "I rather like it." He pulled out the two books he'd stashed under the bench and set them on the table.

For a moment, they just stared at the Books of History. Red twine still bound the black and the brown covers. It was the first time any of the others had laid eyes on the books since Johnis had retrieved them from Teeleh's lair.

"This . . . is what it's all about," Johnis said. His words fell like stones, heavy after the night's celebration.

Silvie stepped forward and touched the leather cover of the book that had come from Teeleh. "All of what we went through, for these books? We nearly gave our lives for them. What would happen if we opened one?"

"We can't!" Johnis said. He still hadn't told them of his horrific

CHOSEN

visions. Too dangerous. And he wasn't convinced they were just visions. "The power is terrible. You saw the look on Teeleh's face."

"There are five more books," Darsal said.

"I don't see how we can find five more books, if the last few days is any measure," Billos said.

Johnis looked up at him. "Do we have a choice?"

"You always have a choice," a voice said on their right. There on the railing perched Michal, the Roush. Gabil floated in on wide white wings and landed delicately on the rail beside Michal.

"Hello, kids," he said. "Care for a karate lesson?"

"Ho, Johnis!" a man cried, walking by. He raised his fist in a salute. "Billos, Darsal, Silvie. Fine job. You can fight by my side anytime. Anytime, I say!"

Johnis dipped his head. "Thank you."

"Yes, thank you, fierce warrior," Gabil cried. "And don't forget that I was there, too, putting the black beasts through this blender called my feet!"

"Gabil . . ." Michal started but then gave up.

The man walked off, grinning, showing no sign that he'd heard Gabil.

"They can't hear you?" Silvie asked.

"Or see us," Michal said. "You're the only four who can. We've always been around. One of these days we'll show you our village."

"You have villages? What about babies?"

"Of course. In the trees." He pointed up.

A lone shriek pierced the air. A Shataiki cry.

257

"Them too?" Billos asked.

"Your eyes have been opened, lad," Michal said. "Just because most people can't see a reality doesn't mean it doesn't exist. The legends are true. I hope I don't have to remind you that you can't speak of this to anyone. Not even Thomas."

"Then what, pray tell, are we supposed to tell them?" Darsal asked. "You want us to lie?"

"Be creative. But you cannot speak of the Black Forests, of the Books of History, or for that matter, of your mission, which is all that matters now."

"You said Black Forests," Johnis said. "As in more than one. We burned the forest to the ground!"

"That you did. It was the smallest forest. It will soon be covered by sand as though it never existed. But there are five more, all much larger. Seven green forests and six black forests."

"And each contains a book?"

"I wish it were that easy," Michal said, sighing. "Unfortunately, I don't have a clue where to send you next."

Gabil sprang from the railing and settled on the table with the books. "Which is just fine—more time for training!"

"Honestly, Gabil," Billos said, grinning, "your moves are made for flying bats. Unless you can teach us to fly, we're at a loss."

"Really? Well, maybe I *can* teach you to fly. It might cause a few bumps and bruises, though. And I can't promise you that you will ever actually fly, but you must learn my karate. If that's the only way . . ."

"Please forgive my friend's eagerness," Michal said. But this time he was smiling. "Now, I suggest you get your story straight and prepare to go after the next book. Gabil, we should get back. We still have wounded to care for."

Gabil fluttered off. "Practice your moves!" he cried. "I'll test you soon."

"Oh," Michal said, turning back. He withdrew something from his belt and set it on the railing. A silver ring. "I almost forgot this. We found it in the desert with a piece of cloth. It was placed there today."

Then he whooshed into the night.

Johnis stepped forward and lifted the ring. He recognized it immediately. "My mother's ring!"

"Your mother's ring?" Silvie said. "Michal wanted you to know that the Horde took it?"

But Johnis didn't think that was what Michal had meant by leaving the ring. His heart pounded, and sweat beaded his forehead. "She's alive."

"I thought she was killed," Billos said.

"They never recovered her body. This means she's alive!"

"You . . . you mean she's a Scab now?"

The possibilities swirled through Johnis's mind. Scab or not, she was his mother, and the thought that she was at this moment alive was almost too much to bear.

He pocketed the ring and faced the other three, jaw set. "I say we make a vow." He placed one Book of History on top of the other and placed his right hand on both. "The balance of power is on our shoulders. This is all that matters now. We take a vow now—all of us or none of us."

"To find the other five books," Silvie said, placing her hand on his.

Darsal walked over and slid her hand over Silvie's. "To fulfill our destiny."

They looked at Billos, but Billos was walking already, eyes on the books. He put his hand on the top and looked Johnis in the eye. "To kill the Horde, slaughter the Shataiki, and find the missing Books of History if it's the last thing we ever do. I vow it."

"I vow it," Darsal said.

"I vow it," Silvie said.

Johnis took a deep breath. "And I vow it."

Their eyes met again, and they nodded at each other in the cool morning darkness.

"Then we live or we die for the Books of History," Johnis said. "Let the quest begin."

THE STORY CONTINUES
WITH *INFIDEL*

There are fifteen missing years between Black and Red in Ted Dekker's epic Circle Series. Missing until now that is. The Lost Books (Chosen, Infidel, Renegade, Chaos, Lunatic, and Elyon) finally reveal the dark secrets of those years. You don't have to read one series before the other, but reading both is the only way to fully enter the Circle.

WITH GREEN,
THE CIRCLE IS NOW COMPLETE

"A FULL-FORCE CLASH BETWEEN GOOD AND EVIL. A TORNADO OF ACTION . . .

CHOSEN

INFIDEL

RENEGADE

TED DEKKER
NEW YORK TIMES BEST-SELLING AUTHOR

THE BEST-SELLING SERIES

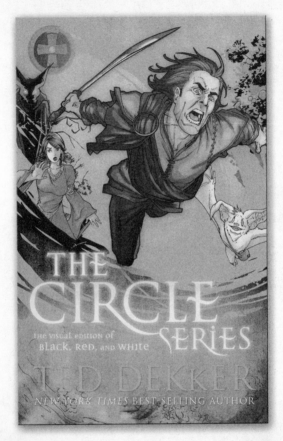

THE LOST BOOKS
GRAPHIC NOVELS

TED DEKKER is the *New York Times* best-selling author of more than twenty novels. He is known for stories that combine adrenaline-laced plots with incredible confrontations between good and evil. He lives in Texas with his wife and children.